# Mallory and the Dream Horse

# Mallory and the Dream Horse
## Ann M. Martin

AN
**APPLE**
PAPERBACK

SCHOLASTIC INC.
New York Toronto London Auckland Sydney

*The author gratefully acknowledges
Jahnna Beecham
and
Malcolm Hillgartner
for their help in
preparing this manuscript.*

Cover art by Hodges Soileau

ISBN 0-590-44965-6

12 11 10 9 8 7 6 5 4 3 2 1                    2 3 4 5 6 7/9

Printed in the U.S.A.                              40

First Scholastic printing, May 1992

# CHAPTER 1

"*Yankee Doodle went to town a-riding on a pony, stuck a feather in his hat and called it Mack and Roni!*"

"Claire," I giggled, "I think it's *macaroni*. You know, like the noodle."

"Noodle!" my sister squealed as she clutched an old mop from the basement. "That's what I'll call my horse."

Claire patted her mop on the head and said, "Good Noodle." Then, singing at the top of her lungs, she galloped around my bedroom.

Well, it's not really *my* bedroom. I share it with Vanessa, another sister of mine. We have to share rooms because there are so many of us Pikes. We have (are you ready for this?) eight kids in our family. Add two adults and you've got a pretty crowded house.

I'm Mallory Pike. I'm eleven and I'm the oldest Pike. Then come the triplets Byron, Adam, and Jordan, who are ten, and Vanessa, who's nine. Nicky's eight, Margo is seven, and Claire is five.

All of us Pike kids have brown hair and blue eyes, but I'm the only one who has curly reddish hair. I am also the only one with braces (lucky me). Plus, I have to wear glasses.

Being the oldest is not as great as it might sound. Lots of times my parents expect me to help out with baby-sitting, which I don't mind doing, but not all the time. For awhile I felt like they were really taking me for granted, but we worked it out, and now they always schedule my sitting jobs just like we do in the BSC.

What's the BSC? It stands for the Baby-sitters Club, which is the greatest group of friends anyone could have. But I'll tell you about that later.

Anyway, it was a Saturday and Jessi Ramsey, my best friend in Stoneybrook, Connecticut (and the world), was at my house for the day. We were doing what we usually do on rainy Saturday afternoons — talking about horses.

Jessi and I *love* horses. In fact you could say we are horse-crazy. We love to read books about horses. Our favorites are those by Marguerite Henry, who wrote *Misty of Chincoteague*. But we'll read any book about a horse. Someday I hope to be a great author and write and illustrate books about horses of all kinds — mustangs, quarterhorses, Appaloosas, Clydesdales, Percherons — you name it. I love them all.

While I would like to be an author, Jessi wants to be a ballerina. And she will be. I'm sure of it. First of all, she's got the perfect dancer's body — slim, long legs, a beautiful neck, and graceful fingers. Second of all, she has already danced several leading roles in ballets in nearby Stamford. We (the rest of the BSC and I) always go to her performances, and boy is she good.

Jessica (that's her formal name) has a younger sister, Becca, short for Rebecca, and a baby brother, John Philip Ramsey, Jr., which is a very big name for such a little guy. Everyone calls him Squirt. Jessi's Aunt Cecelia lives with her family, too. So altogether the Ramseys have six people living in their house. We have ten. That's one of the main differences between me and Jessi. Also, Jessi is black and I'm white. It doesn't matter to me, but it did to some people in town when the Ramseys first moved to Stoneybrook. They really had a tough time in the beginning, but that's all in the past. Now things are much better for Jessi and her family.

Anyway, Jessi was lying on my bed with one of her legs extended in the air. It nearly touched her ear. (Ow!) Jessi always does stretching exercises when she's sitting around so that she'll stay limber for ballet. I've gotten so used to it that I hardly notice it anymore. She was reading *Misty of Chincoteague* again and I was sitting cross-legged on the floor, reading the ending of *Black Beauty* for the two hundredth time, when Claire burst into the room, straddling her mop.

"Whoa! Whoa!" I said, after she'd circled the room several times. When Claire pulled her mop (I mean, horse) to a stop, I asked, "What are you doing riding Noodle in the house?"

"I'm practicing for the circus. I'm the bareback rider." Claire pointed proudly at the mop handle. "See? No saddle."

"I think your horse could use some more oats," Jessi said, trying to keep a straight face. "He's kind of skinny."

Claire put her hands on her hips, and her mop-horse clattered to the ground. "He is not. He's perfect."

"Claire," I said, pointing to the mop lying on the rug, "you dropped your horse."

Claire looked at the mop and declared, "Noodle is resting. He's very sleepy." She stifled a yawn as she spoke.

My parents were home, so I wasn't officially on baby-sitting duty, but I knew when Claire needed a nap. I picked up Noodle in one hand and guided Claire out of the room. "Meet me in the rec room," I called to Jessi over my shoulder. "We'll make popcorn and watch *The Black Stallion* again."

"Great!" she replied. *The Black Stallion* is one of our absolute favorite movies.

"But I have to practice my riding," Claire protested feebly as I helped her onto her bed.

"Noodle's too tired," I explained, laying the mop on the floor beside my sister's bed. "He just needs a quick nap and then he'll be ready to do higher leaps and gallop even faster around the ring."

"You really think so?" she murmured, snuggling her head into her pillow.

"I know so." I draped a light quilt over Claire and then tiptoed out the door and down the stairs. It was very quiet upstairs, but downstairs was a different story.

Vanessa, Margo, and Nicky were playing so loudly in the dining room that it was hard for Jessi and me to hear our movie in the rec room. Finally we just turned down the volume and talked about our favorite subject: horses.

"Okay," Jessi announced as she stretched her legs out to the side, practically in a split. (Double ow!) "If you could pick your dream horse, what would it be?"

"Oh, boy." I sank back in the overstuffed

chair by the television and thought for a second. "He'd have to be an Arabian. They're the nicest. A pure white one with a long flowing mane and warm brown eyes."

"A pure white Arabian," Jessi sighed. "That sounds wonderful."

"He'd be extremely smart, so if I fell off his back and broke my ankle in the woods, he'd know to go get help."

Jessi chuckled. "Just like Lassie."

I tossed a pillow at Jessi. "You know what I mean."

Jessi grinned. "Mine would do cute things like bring me his bridle and count to ten with his hoof."

"Mine would live in a stable in my backyard and we'd go riding every day. And we'd enter horse shows all over the country and win."

"But you'd have to know how to ride first," Jessi reminded me.

"Well, of course I'd take lessons," I said. "As many as I wanted and as often as I liked."

It's funny. Both Jessi and I dream of having our own horse and riding every day, but neither one of us has ever had even one lesson.

"Remember that old movie with Shirley Temple called *The Little Princess*?" Jessi stretched forward and put her elbows on the floor. "She played a rich girl named Sara

6

Crewe in Victorian England who had her own pony."

I nodded. "And she went riding every day." I leaned back and sighed. "I'd give anything to be Sara Crewe and have my own horse."

"Me, too," Jessi murmured.

I sat up and squeezed my eyes closed. "All right. I'm going to count to ten, and when I open my eyes I'll have my dream horse, riding lessons, and contact lenses."

Jessi squeezed her own eyes shut. "When *I* open my eyes, I'll have my dream horse, riding lessons, and I will dance the role of the Sugar Plum Fairy in *The Nutcracker* next Christmas."

We held our breath and started counting, but before we could reach ten, Nicky burst into the room, wearing a pair of swim trunks. An old pink bathroom rug was draped across one shoulder. He'd pinned big black construction paper spots onto the rug to make it look like leopard fur. He pounded his chest with his fists and let out a deafening yodel. "I'm Tarzan, King of the Apes, and I can wrestle alligators."

"Nicky!" I protested. "Can't you see we're doing something very important here?"

Nicky's shoulders slumped and I felt awful. "But that's okay," I added. "Because I have never even seen an alligator, let alone one that wrestles. Where is it?"

Nicky cupped his hands around his mouth and let out another loud yodel. Margo entered the room, a bed sheet wrapped around her shoulders. She held our hamster Frodo cupped in her hands. Frodo had a little green felt cape tied around his shoulders and didn't look very happy about-it.

"Here's the ferocious alligator, Tarzan," Margo said, handing the hamster to Nicky.

Nicky clutched the animal to his chest and said, "Thank you, Margo the Magnificent."

"Margo the Magnificent?" Jessi repeated.

"Yes!" Margo grandly swept her bed sheet over one shoulder. "I am the world's greatest magician," she announced. "I can turn apples into oranges and lots of other things into ordinary household items. Want to see?"

Jessi and I looked at each other and tried not to giggle. Margo sounded like a television commercial.

"Wait a minute!" Nicky bellowed. "First they're going to watch me wrestle Frodo — I mean, the vicious alligator." He dropped onto his knees and tried to make Frodo sit still on the carpet.

Margo ignored him and pulled an apple out of her sheet, then set it on the coffee table. "This is just an ordinary apple,"she said. "I

8

simply wave my magic cape across it — "

I bit my lip to keep from laughing as Margo struggled to hold the sheet in the air while she switched the apple with an orange that was hidden beneath her other arm. The orange slipped out of her fingers onto the rug and rolled toward the hamster, who bolted out of the way beneath the couch.

"Oh, shoot," Margo muttered. "I keep messing that part up."

"Now look what you did!" Nicky shouted. "My gator's escaped."

"Never fear, Reena's here," Vanessa cried from the doorway. She was dressed in a pink leotard and tights. "I walk the high wire at the top of the tent. I carry a pole that is straight, not bent." Vanessa writes poetry and likes to rhyme when she talks. She rolled a strip of pale blue ribbon out in front of her and pretended to walk along it, carrying a broom as a balance stick.

"Give me that stick," Nicky said, gesturing for his sister to hand him the broom. "I'll nudge Frodo and get him out from under the couch."

Vanessa executed a perfect turn on the ribbon and headed back to the door. "As soon as I get off the wire, I'll give you my pole," she called over her shoulder.

"No, I need it now." He grabbed Vanessa

around the waist, and she wobbled wildly from side to side.

"Don't do that, Nicky!" she cried. "Can't you see I'm working without a net? Stop!"

The two of them tumbled onto the carpet in a tangle of knees and elbows. While they wrestled, Margo continued to struggle with her disappearing orange trick.

Jessi doubled over with laughter.

"What's so funny?" I called over the racket.

"Your family," she replied. "It's like a looney bin in here."

Then Claire galloped into the room on her mop-horse Noodle, her eyes still puffy with sleep. "Is it showtime?" she cried. "Why didn't somebody tell me?"

As Claire rode her horse into the chaos, I grinned and shouted back to Jessi, "Make that a three-ring circus. The Pike Family presents The Craziest Show on Earth."

# CHAPTER 2

It was almost five o'clock on Monday when I realized that no one in my family had picked up the mail. Usually Margo and Nicky fight over who gets to bring it from the mailbox, but they were in the backyard inventing new talents to show each other.

The mailbox was filled with the usual stuff — a few bills, a couple of catalogs, a yellow envelope from a sweepstakes place that read, "*You* could be a winner!" and a flier for a sale at the local supermarket. I was just about to drop it all on the table by the front door when a green-and-white brochure slipped out and fluttered to the floor.

I bent over to pick it up and couldn't believe my eyes. There was a picture of an elegant thoroughbred and an equestrian dressed in English riding clothes. They were posed beside a ring made of rails and posts painted a crisp white.

" 'Horseback Riding Lessons, English Style,' " I read out loud. "Classes starting soon at Kendallwood Farm, Connecticut's finest riding school." I looked at the address and gasped. Kendallwood was on the outskirts of Stoneybrook, just an easy bike trip from my house. "This is wonderful!" I exclaimed "I can ride a horse without owning one. Every week!"

I clutched the brochure to my chest and spun in a circle, not knowing whether to race through the house looking for my mother, or run to the phone to call Jessi. Luckily, before I did any of those things, I glanced at the clock on our mantel. It said ten after five.

"The Baby-sitters Club!" I gasped. Our meetings start promptly at five-thirty every Monday, Wednesday, and Friday afternoon at Claudia Kishi's house. If I hopped on my bike and left that instant I would have a few minutes before the meeting began to tell Jessi about my wonderful discovery.

I carefully tucked the brochure in my jacket, grabbed my bike, and pedaled as fast as I could to Claud's house.

This is probably a good time to tell you about the Baby-sitters Club and how it got started. There are seven of us in the club. Jessi and I are the youngest (we're in sixth grade) so we're called junior officers. The other five members are Kristy Thomas, Claudia Kishi, Mary Anne Spier, Stacey McGill, and Dawn Schafer. They are thirteen and in eighth grade.

It was Kristy's idea to start the club, which is probably why she is also the president. Kristy got her great idea over a year ago when her mother couldn't find a sitter for her younger brother, David Michael. Kristy listened to her mother dial number after number with no luck. And that's when the brilliant idea hit.

"Why not have one number where a parent can reach several sitters at one time?" Kristy thought. So she talked to Mary Anne, Claudia, and eventually Stacey. Together they made up advertising fliers and passed them out to everyone they knew. They decided to hold meetings in Claudia's room, since she has a phone of her own. And soon the calls were pouring in! In fact, things grew so busy that they decided to add a few more people — Dawn, Jessi, and me. Now we have even added associate officers, Logan Bruno and Shannon Kilbourne. They don't attend meetings, but they're ready to fill in if the rest of us are busy.

Our meetings are half an hour long. Dues are collected by Stacey on Mondays —the money is for fun things like club parties and sleepovers. It also helps to cover Claud's phone bill and to replace items in our Kid-Kits.

What are Kid-Kits? Just another one of Kristy's brilliant ideas. (She's got a million of them!) Each of us found a cardboard carton that we decorated with paint and fabric and other art supplies that Claudia gave us. Then we filled the boxes with toys, crayons, puppets, and games from our own houses. Kristy figured that children would much rather play with somebody else's toys than their own. And she was right! The kids love them.

Another great idea of Kristy's is the club notebook. It's like a daily diary in which we write up each job that we go on. It's really useful because we find out if a kid has developed a new fear, or is having trouble at school, or is allergic to something and needs to take medication. Some of the members think writing in the notebook is a pain, but I really like it.

Each member of the BSC is a real individual, which I think makes for a perfect club. Kristy, our president, is outgoing and filled with terrific ideas. Her mom was divorced but then she married Watson Brewer, a genuine millionaire, and the Thomases moved to this huge mansion across town from the rest of us. Now, in addition to her three brothers she has a stepbrother, stepsister, and an adopted sister.

Kristy doesn't care a whole lot about how she looks and generally can be found wearing jeans, sneakers, a turtleneck shirt, and a sweater (it's almost like her uniform). Kristy's big love is sports, which is why she coaches a junior softball team called Kristy's Krushers.

Mary Anne Spier is our club secretary and Kristy's best friend. But the two of them couldn't be more different. While Kristy is outgoing, Mary Anne is very shy. Her mom died when Mary Anne was a baby, so her father raised her all by himself. (He used to be really strict and not let her wear anything too adult, but that's changed. And boy, is Mary Anne relieved!) Mary Anne is also very emotional. She cries at the drop of a hat. I'm not kidding. I've even seen her cry at a sad TV commercial. And she's a romantic. In fact, Mary Anne was the first one of us in the BSC to have a steady boyfriend. (Logan Bruno. He's one of the associate officers I told you about.) Besides being Kristy's best friend, Mary Anne is also Dawn Schafer's best friend. And stepsister. It was really strange how that happened.

You see, Dawn used to live in California, but when her parents got a divorce, her mom decided to move Dawn and her brother Jeff back to the town where she grew up. So that brought Dawn — with her waist-length blonde hair, blue eyes, and perfect skin — to Stoneybrook.

Dawn dresses in her own unique style — we call it California casual. Plus, she is a total health food nut. The sight of a hamburger makes her gag. And she loves mysteries and ghost stories. That's why it was absolutely perfect when her mom bought this neat old colonial farmhouse that actually has a secret passageway in it.

Soon Dawn and Mary Anne became friends at school. Then they discovered that Mary Anne's dad and Dawn's mom had been high school sweethearts. Can you believe it? So, of course, the two of them decided to get Mr. Spier and Mrs. Schafer back together. It worked like a charm. They fell in love all over again, got married, and that's how Dawn and Mary Anne ended up as stepsisters.

Oh, one more thing. I told you Mary Anne and Logan Bruno were dating. Well, Dawn is now dating Logan's cousin, Lewis. Sort of. It's hard to call it dating since he lives in Louisville, Kentucky. But they write each other and, as Dawn says, they *definitely* have a strong friendship.

There are two more members of the BSC: Claudia Kishi, vice-president, and Stacey McGill, treasurer. They are also best friends. Claudia is Japanese-American and drop-dead gorgeous. And artsy. She makes her own earrings and tie-dyes her own T-shirts. Claudia can put together strange combinations of clothes — like one of her father's old shirts over tie-dyed tights, with a big belt and a funky vest — and look like she stepped out of a fashion magazine. She's not a great student, but she more than makes up for it in talent. Her parents think she just needs to apply herself to her schoolwork, but I think part of her problem is that her older sister, Janine, is a major brain. I mean, we're talking genius. I think Claud figures that since Janine has taken care of the brains category, she'll concentrate on art. And boy, does she ever. Pottery, drawing, painting, sculpting — you name it, Claud can do it.

She does have one flaw. She's a junk food addict. At every BSC meeting you can count on Claudia to have a bag of red hots, Mallomars, or potato chips for us to chow down. All of us except Dawn, who turns up her nose at candy, and Stacey, who can't eat sweets.

Stacey is diabetic, which means her body is unable to process sugar. She has to give herself these shots (ew, ick) every day. Stacey is also the ultimate in cool. She used to live in New York City, so she is very sophisticated. Claud calls her the Queen of Dibbleness, which is our word for ultra cool. Stacey perms her thick blonde hair and wears sparkly nail polish and earrings that Claudia designs. She's very pretty but a little on the thin side. That probably has a lot to do with her strict diet. Can you imagine always having to count calories and monitor your sugar intake and give yourself injections? I couldn't do it. No way. But Stacey seems to manage all right and stay cheerful about it, too.

So those are my friends. The people who have helped me through the crises in my life — like when my dad lost his job. They've also shared my successes — like when I won the award for Best Overall Fiction at Young Author's Day at school. Now I couldn't wait to tell them about horseback riding lessons at Kendallwood.

It was five-twenty by the time I reached Claud's house. I didn't even ring the doorbell but raced upstairs to her room. Kristy was already leaning back in the director's chair, her visor on her head and a pencil over one ear. Claud was rummaging through her desk drawers, looking for a bag of candy kisses that she'd snuck into her room when her mom wasn't looking. Jessi had arrived a minute ahead of me and was just taking off her jean jacket.

"Jessi!" I could barely keep from shouting. "It's happened. My dream has come true!"

Jessi blinked at me, mystified. "You won a million dollars?"

"No." I chuckled. "Look." I thrust the brochure into her hands, and while she read it, I said excitedly, "Well, not my whole dream. I mean, I don't have my own private horse and stables and riding lessons. But this is the next best thing."

Kristy leaned forward in her chair while Claudia stopped her candy search to stare at me. I tried to explain. "See, Jessi and I decided we wanted to be just like Sara Crewe, who is really Shirley Temple in the movie called *The Little Princess*."

"This is going over my head," Kristy said, turning to Claud. "How about you?"

Claud shrugged. "She's totally lost me."

I realized I wasn't making any sense. So I took a deep breath and tried once more. "Jessi and I want a horse. We also want to take riding lessons. Well, I got this brochure that says Kendallwood Farm is offering riding lessons. They're just on the edge of town and" — I pointed to the price — "they're not too expensive."

Jessi's brown eyes shone as she raised her head and grinned at me. "I'm going to sign up for lessons, too."

"We could do it together." I squeezed her arm happily. "Wouldn't that be fun?"

A slight frown crossed Jessi's brow. "Of course, I'll have to talk to my parents first."

"Oh, me too," I said. "But they'll say yes. They just have to."

"All in favor?" Kristy lifted her pencil like a gavel.

Jessi and I smiled at each other and shouted, "Aye!"

"Opposed?"

Claudia looked under the bed as a joke and shook her head. Kristy tapped her pencil on the desk. "Then it's settled. You'll both take horseback riding lessons."

At that moment the numbers on Claudia's digital clock switched from 5:28 to 5:29. The door opened and Dawn and Mary Anne rushed into the room, followed by Stacey. They called hellos to everyone and took their seats. Jessi and I dropped onto the floor at the foot of the bed as the clock numbers switched to five-thirty — and the meeting began.

I barely remember it because all I could think about was riding lessons at Kendallwood. The phone rang quite a few times as people called to arrange for sitters. In between calls, Stacey collected our dues, which she put in a manila envelope. Mary Anne diligently recorded the jobs in the record book as they were arranged.

I landed a job sitting for Nina and Eleanor Marshall on Wednesday afternoon; Stacey got a weekend job with the Arnold twins; and then Kristy, Jessi, Claudia, and Dawn each booked jobs. But I have to admit I wasn't paying any attention by that time. I was still thinking about the thoroughbred in the brochure. I pictured myself perched on his back, looking elegant in my red riding coat, hunt cap, and long black boots.

Before I knew it, it was six o'clock and Kristy was waving her hand in front of my face. "Yoo-hoo, pardner!"

"Pardner?" I repeated, blinking my eyes in confusion. "What are you talking about?"

"Mal has returned to the planet," Kristy cried triumphantly. Then she put her hands on her hips and said, "I've only been calling your name for the last three minutes. Where've you been?"

"Sorry," I said, blushing. "I guess I was daydreaming about riding."

"Well, in case you haven't noticed," Kristy said, pointing to the clock, "the meeting's over. Time to saddle up your horse and head back to the corral."

Kristy grinned at the rest of the club members, who began to laugh. Even though the joke was on me, I think I was the one laughing the hardest.

# CHAPTER 3

*Ding-dong!*

I pressed the bell at the Marshalls' house Wednesday afternoon, and the door swung open before the ringing had stopped.

"Mallory! Hooray! You're here." Four-year-old Nina Marshall stood smiling in the doorway. "Come on in, but be careful not to step on Blankie."

"Blankie" was a huge grayish baby blanket that was draped over Nina's arm and was being dragged on the floor beside her. The edges were frayed where the satin border used to be. I realized that the blanket had once been pale blue, but lots of use and probably hundreds of washings had given it the faded gray color.

"Hi, Mallory," Mrs. Marshall called from the kitchen. "I've just put two pot pies in the oven for the girls for dinner. They'll be done around five o'clock. Eleanor is taking a nap but she should be getting up any time now."

"How are her ears?" I recalled that Eleanor had suffered from ear infections when she was younger. I'd had to give her medicine for them many times.

"They're just fine." Mrs. Marshall smiled, pleased that I had remembered to ask. "I think now that she's two, we're past all that."

I watched Nina cross into the den, dragging Blankie behind her. She called over her shoulder, "Come play Barbies with me, Mallory."

Mrs. Marshall smiled at her daughter and then turned back to me. "Nina just started preschool," she said in a confidential tone of voice. "The children attend three times a week, and today was her second day."

"Oh? How'd it go?" I remembered watching my brothers and sisters go off to their first days at school, and how scared and excited they had been.

Mrs. Marshall pursed her lips. "I can't really tell. Normally, she's very talkative, but she's kept awfully quiet about this."

"Come on, Mallory!" Nina called from the den.

Her mother chuckled. "You two have a good time. I'll be back in a couple of hours."

I waved good-bye to Mrs. Marshall and, after checking to make sure Eleanor was still sleeping soundly upstairs, joined Nina in the den. She had laid two Barbie dolls and a pile of clothes on the floor.

I picked up one of the dolls and set it on my lap. "How about if we pretend that Barbie is going to her first day of school, just like you did?"

Nina blinked her blue eyes at me and shrugged. "Okay, if you want."

"Sure. School can be fun." I chose a pair of red-and-white-striped tights and a long top made of sweat shirt material for my doll. (Claud would have been proud.) As Nina dressed her Barbie, I asked gently, "Have you had fun at school, Nina?"

Nina shrugged once more. "I don't know."

I tried another question. "What did you and your friends do today?"

Nina was busy putting a long sequined gown on her doll, so she didn't look up when she said, "I don't have any friends."

I walked my doll across the carpet to her and pretended to make her talk. "Oh, Nina, you'll have lots of friends. It's only your second day of school."

Nina walked her doll toward mine. "It doesn't matter what day it is," she said. "I won't ever have any friends."

Hmm. "Gosh, Nina, don't you like the kids at school?" I made Barbie say.

Nina walked her Barbie doll to a big pink

plastic car and put her inside it. "Some of them. But they don't like me."

"Oh, I bet that's not true."

"It is so." This time Nina's lower lip stuck out in a pout that looked like she was dangerously close to tears. "They don't like me *or* Blankie."

"Blankie?" I pushed my glasses up on my nose and looked at the drab old blanket that lay across Nina's lap. "You take Blankie to school?"

Nina nodded vigorously. "Blankie goes everywhere with me."

I could just imagine Nina dragging that big old faded blanket to school and what the other kids must have thought about it. I asked in my gentlest voice, "Do the kids tease you?"

"Maybe." Nina's voice was barely audible. She picked up the blanket and held one frayed corner against her cheek and the other part under her arm, as if she were protecting it.

I knew how much Nina liked her Blankie, but I also knew how cruel kids can be. I tried to suggest some solutions to her problem.

"Blankie is such a big blanket. Have you thought about taking a different blanket to school with you? One that's smaller?"

Nina's eyes widened in horror at the idea of a substitute. "No, I want my *real* Blankie. He goes everywhere with me."

"Maybe you could take Blankie to school but leave him in your cubby."

"No, he'd be lonely." She hugged the blanket even closer to her, as if she thought someone might try to steal it from her.

I hated to admit it, but I was stumped. It looked like Nina and her blanket would never be separated, so I gave up trying. Anyway, at that moment I could hear Eleanor in her crib upstairs.

"Nap done!" she shouted from her room. "Mommy! Nap done!"

I placed my doll back in her case and stood up. "I'll get Eleanor and then why don't the three of us go outside and play?"

Nina's face brightened in a sunny smile. "That sounds like fun." She returned her doll and the clothes to their case and began busily putting them in her wicker toy chest.

Eleanor was standing in her crib when I reached her room. Her hair was sticking out in all directions and she had that big-eyed look of surprise that little kids have when they first wake up.

"Hi, Eleanor," I said, smoothing her hair. "It's me — Mallory."

She tried to repeat my name but what came out sounded more like "Mow-ee."

I lifted her out of her crib and, as I changed

her diaper, asked, "Would you like to go outside and swing?"

She rubbed the sleep from her eyes with the back of her fist and grinned. "Outside. Swing."

Nina and Blankie met us at the back door and the three of us went outside. The Marshalls had set up a swing with a slide in their backyard. Eleanor made a beeline for it as soon as I opened the back door. Nina followed right behind her, still clutching the big gray blanket.

Eleanor stood by the swing and held out her arms to me. "Up. Please." I lifted her into the swing and we watched as Nina and Blankie made their way up the steps of the slide. The blanket was so big that Nina could hardly hold onto the railing as she climbed.

"How is Blankie going to go down the slide?" I called as I gave Eleanor a gentle push in the swing.

"We go down together." Nina lay the blanket across the slide, then sat in the middle of it and wrapped herself up as if she were in a sleeping bag. "It makes you go real fast."

She was right. Nina whizzed down the metal slide and rocketed off the bottom, landing (luckily) in a soft mound of grass. Then she untangled herself from the blanket and raced for the swing next to Eleanor's.

"How is Blankie going to get on the swing with you?" I asked.

"Easy." Nina folded the blanket into a long shawl and wrapped it around her shoulders so that she looked like a football player with padding around her neck. Then she backed toward the swing and sat down.

"That's amazing," I said. Nina had obviously had a lot of practice with Blankie, and it was easy to see how tough it was going to be for her to leave her "friend" at home.

The timer went off in the kitchen and I clapped my hands together. "Chow time!"

Eleanor, Nina, and Blankie (I was now starting to think of Blankie as a third person) raced for the back door of the house. The kids took up their positions around the kitchen table, with Blankie sitting in his own chair this time, next to Nina. I served them their pot pies, and they were still eating when Mrs. Marshall came home.

As she looked through her wallet, I cleared my throat, all set to tell her about Nina's possible trouble at school. But then I noticed the clock in the hall. I only had five minutes to get to the BSC meeting! (Did I tell you how strict Kristy is about starting on time? She absolutely hates it when any of us is late.) I decided I'd have to talk to Mrs. Marshall about Nina's Blankie problem another time. I ran all the way from Rosedale, where the Marshalls live, to Claud's house on Bradford Court.

It's a good thing I did get there on time because the phone started ringing nonstop the moment our meeting began. Every single member of the BSC booked a job. In fact, we were so busy we even had to call one of our associates to see if he could take a Wednesday afternoon job. Mary Anne volunteered to make that call.

"I'll phone Logan," she said, already dialing his number. "I don't think he's busy on Wednesday."

"You never know," Claud teased. "He may have a date or something."

Mary Anne stuck out her tongue at Claudia, but before she could say anything, Logan answered the phone. While Mary Anne made arrangements with him to take the Wednesday afternoon job, Jessi whispered to me, "Have you talked to your parents yet about riding lessons?"

I shook my head. "Tonight's the night. I've been working on a strategy."

"Strategy?" Jessi raised one eyebrow.

"Sure. I can't ask about something as important as riding lessons without having worked out the details first. Dad will ask a lot of questions, and I have to be ready with answers."

Jessi grinned and shook her head. "Mal, you amaze me. I was just planning to ask my parents straight out."

"That might work, too."

Mary Anne had hung up the phone, and now Kristy was making an announcement about buying new items for our Kid-Kits, so I quickly whispered, "No matter what happens tonight, I'll call you."

"Right!"

# CHAPTER 4

Dinner at the Pike house can be pretty crazy at times, and Wednesday night was no exception. Nicky and Margo started a kicking war under the table, which ended with Margo in tears and Nicky banished to the other end of the kitchen. The triplets kept spooning mashed potatoes into their mouths and showing me what that looked like. I wanted to yell at them, but I had to keep a cool head. Tonight was the night I planned to ask my parents about taking riding lessons.

My mom had just finished wiping up Claire's spilled milk when my sister knocked her glass over again. I leaped to my feet and cried, "I'll clean it up this time, Mom. You stay there."

"Thanks, Mallory." My mother leaned back in her chair with a sigh of relief. "Now isn't that nice?" she asked the table in general. "Life would be a lot easier around here if you all followed your sister's example."

My father, who'd seemed totally oblivious to everything that had been going on during dinner, looked up from his roast beef. "I think Mallory wants something."

Sometimes I'd swear my dad can read minds. I didn't think I had been that obvious.

"Every time Mal gets extra helpful," my father continued, "it means she's about to ask for something," he said to my mother.

I thought back to the time I had asked to get my ears pierced and remembered that I'd done a major cleanup job that night, too.

"Okay, you caught me," I admitted. "But what I want to ask is really important to me. Probably the most important thing in the world — so I want you to be in a good mood."

Jordan chose that moment to press his fingers against Adam's cheeks. A cloud of mashed potatoes exploded across the table.

"Oh, gross!" Vanessa screamed, pulling tiny bits of potato out of her hair.

"Jordan!" my father said in his sternest voice. "That is *not* acceptable behavior. One more stunt like that and you'll spend the rest of the evening in your room."

"But Dad," Jordan said in a hurt voice, "Adam's the one who kept stuffing potatoes into his mouth."

Mom closed her eyes briefly. "I don't care,"

she said. "Now stop playing with your food and finish your dinner."

I shot my brothers the most disgusted look I could muster and then turned back to my father. "As I was saying before we were so *rudely* interrupted, these riding lessons mean more to me than anything."

"Riding lessons," my mother repeated as she busily wiped Adam's mashed potatoes off the drinking glasses and serving bowls. "That's the first I've heard of this."

"A flier came in the mail on Monday," I explained. "I've spent the last few days trying to arrange my schedule so the lessons won't interfere with anything. Just a minute."

I hurried into the hall to the front closet, where I had placed the chart I'd drawn the night before.

"Visual aids," my father said, chuckling, as I returned carrying the white poster board. "Very impressive."

"Thanks." I beamed at my father. I knew I'd scored a big point. "I want you to know that I've thought about this quite carefully."

My chart was really a graph, with the days of the week listed along the side and times of the day listed across the top.

"See, I've put in all of the BSC meetings on Mondays, Wednesdays, and Fridays," I explained, "an hour and a half each night for homework, my once-a-month visit to the orthodontist, and" — I put special emphasis on this part — "*my duties at home*. I could easily take the beginner's riding class. It's at ten o'clock on Saturday mornings. I'll just get up an hour earlier to do my chores."

My father wiped his mouth with his napkin and pushed his chair slightly away from the table. "That's fine, but what's this going to cost?"

I knew that sooner or later we'd get around to the bottom line. I gulped and told them the price, quickly adding, "But it's a bargain compared to other stables. And because it's so close, you wouldn't have to drive me. I could ride my bike."

"Hmm." My mother stood up and started clearing the table. I decided to wait until all of my brothers and sisters had left the dining room. Then I'd hit my parents with the next step of my bargaining strategy.

Bargaining is a skill that I'm just starting to learn. Once I went to this flea market and saw this really neat old jewelry box. The price was $7.50, which I thought was too high, so I offered the man $3.75, which I knew was too low. The owner and I finally agreed on a middle price — $4.75 — which was just right. I also used bargaining when I got my ears pierced. I asked my parents for everything —

contact lenses, a new wardrobe, a haircut, and pierced ears, knowing they'd never go for it all. When they finally agreed to a haircut and pierced ears, Mom and Dad thought they had saved themselves a ton of money. Which they had. Only they didn't know that all I really wanted was the pierced ears. The haircut was a bonus. I know it sounds sneaky, but it wasn't. Exactly.

I had told my parents the full price for the riding lessons. I waited till we'd loaded the dishwasher and Dad was drinking a cup of coffee before I made my next offer.

"I know that riding lessons cost a lot of money, especially with eight kids in our family." I didn't mention the added hardship of when my dad had been out of work and we had to use up a lot of our savings. "But I figure that if *I* pay for half of the lessons out of my baby-sitting money, then they really won't even cost as much as Jordan's piano lessons."

My mother and father exchanged glances that showed they were considering the idea. That's when I hit them with my final offer. "It wouldn't have to be for the whole year. Just the beginners course — eight lessons."

"Well." My father took a sip of his coffee and thought for a moment. "If it's what you really want . . ."

That's when I lost my cool. I sprang out of

my chair and wrapped my arms around my father's neck, nearly knocking his coffee cup out of his hands. "It's what I want more than anything in the world. Please! Oh please, oh please!"

My mother laughed at the sight of my father trying to juggle his coffee and hug me at the same time.

Even Dad was chuckling when he said, "Okay, Mallory, you have our permission."

"Since it's only for eight lessons," my mother added. Then she said, "But you really will have to pay for half of it. We can't afford it otherwise. Are you sure you want to do that? That would use up most of the money you've saved from baby-sitting."

"I don't care!" I danced happily around the room. "I'm going to learn how to ride. At last!"

"Then it's settled," my father declared, sounding a lot like Kristy at the Monday meeting. "You're taking riding lessons."

"Yippee! I have to call Jessi right away."

I took the stairs three at a time and nearly broke my leg tripping over the phone cord at the landing. I was so excited that my hands shook as I dialed her number.

"Jessi!" I shrieked into the phone, when she answered. "I get to take horseback riding. They said yes!"

"That's great, Mal."

Jessi's voice sounded oddly flat. I asked worriedly, "Did you talk to your parents?"

"Yes. And they said no."

Then I understood why she didn't sound very happy about my good news.

"Didn't you tell them how much the lessons mean to us — I mean, you?"

Jessi gave a tired sigh. "Yes. But they pointed out that my ballet lessons and baby-sitting already take up most of my time. They think horseback riding would just be too much."

"That's awful, Jessi."

I felt bad for my friend. But I also felt bad for me. I'd had these wonderful visions of the two of us, best friends, riding our horses around the ring, winning medals at riding competitions.

"Listen," Jessi said after a long silence, "I better go. I have a lot of homework to do."

I hung up the phone but barely had time to think about how disappointed Jessi must be, because I was surrounded by four Pike kids, all shouting at once.

"Guess what, Mal, guess what!" Margo squealed. "We're going to put on a talent show."

"But you did that on Saturday, didn't you?" I said, trying to set the phone back on its cradle.

"That was just for you and Jessi," Vanessa said. "And anyway it was more of a circus. This one is going to be a real talent show for the entire neighborhood."

Margo tugged on the sleeve of my T-shirt. "We'll hold auditions and everything."

"Just like *Star Search*," Nicky added.

Vanessa showed me a yellow sign-up sheet. "We'll choose the best acts and then put the show together."

"Of course we four get to be in it," Margo explained, "because we thought of it."

"It'll be the biggest thing that ever hit our neighborhood," Nicky said, giving Claire a high five.

Half of me was still thinking about Jessi, and how awful it was that her parents had said no. The other half was trying to imagine how four small children would manage to hold auditions, organize rehearsals, and get all those kids to show up for the performance. But I didn't want to sound discouraging.

"That's a terrific idea," I said brightly. "I hope you guys can do it."

Margo folded her arms firmly across her chest. "We *will* do it."

I hate to admit it, but at the time I honestly thought their talent show would never *ever* be put on.

# CHAPTER 5

"I'm Lauren Kendall," the riding instructor announced in her clipped British accent. "And I'd like to welcome all of you to Kendallwood Farm."

Saturday had finally arrived, and I was about to begin my first riding lesson. I couldn't believe it. I, Mallory Pike, was standing in a riding ring, holding the reins of a beautiful chestnut mare named Isabelle. I wanted to pinch myself to make sure this wasn't just a dream. Around me in a semicircle were five other new riders, each holding the reins of their horses while we hung on our instructor's every word.

Lauren Kendall was tall and slender, with straight dark hair that she wore pulled back in a silver barrette at her neck. You could tell she spent a lot of time in the sun because her face was deeply tanned, with little smile lines around her sparkling green eyes. In her En-

39

glish riding togs — black boots, tan pants, white blouse, and fitted green jacket — Lauren Kendall looked like she had just stepped off the cover of *Horse and Rider* magazine. I thought she was the coolest person I'd ever seen. I made a silent vow to be just like her when I grew up.

"I'm calling today's lesson 'Taking the Reins,' " Lauren said. "We'll learn how to mount and dismount safely, and how to walk and trot."

All in one lesson? I thought. Goose bumps immediately rippled up my arms. I imagined myself as an accomplished horsewoman — jumping, doing dressage, riding in shows, maybe competing at the Kensington Stakes someday. My horse, Isabelle, seemed to sense my excitement. She flared her nostrils and snorted several times.

"All right, class." Lauren stepped to the center of the ring and tapped her riding crop against the side of her tall boots. "Let's form a circle and lead your horses round the ring by the reins."

As I walked my horse into place behind the one in front of me, I had my first good look at the rest of the kids in my class. I had been too excited to pay much attention to them before. There were four boys and seven other girls. The girl leading the bay ahead of me, a blonde who looked about my age or a little older, caught my eye and I smiled shyly.

She didn't smile back but just raised an eyebrow and murmured, "Nice outfit."

I looked down at my clothes and then back at the class. I could feel my face heat up as I realized that my outfit was completely out of place. Lauren Kendall had told me on the phone to wear an English riding habit if I had one, but if I didn't, just to make sure to wear boots, a helmet, and gloves. And that's what I had done. I had put on my red plaid shirt and jeans (that looked great when I wore them trail riding at Camp Mohawk) and a weathered pair of winter boots. I did have an old riding helmet that my mom had borrowed from one of her friends, but it looked like it had been run over by a herd of horses. My gloves were a worn out leather pair that my dad said he didn't need anymore.

This wouldn't have been so bad if someone else had been dressed like me, but the others were wearing full English riding habits, just like Lauren's. They had on the same tight tan riding pants, and most of the girls wore blouses with high collars. (I read in a magazine that those shirts are called ratcatchers, which is a pretty weird name but seemed kind of perfect for the snooty girl in front of me.) Plus, they were wearing the same high black boots, and velvet riding helmets, which are called hunt caps. As we completed our circle, I forced myself to fix my attention on Lauren.

You're here to learn to ride, I told myself. Not to enter a fashion contest, so just forget about the others.

"That's fine," Lauren said. "Now move to the left side of your horse and prepare to mount up."

I circled Isabelle, making sure to pat her nose and whisper, "Good girl." Then I slipped my left foot in the narrow stirrup and swung my right leg over Isabelle's back.

I felt as if I were sitting on top of the world. I'd ridden Western style before, but that felt so clunky compared to sitting on this English saddle. Now there was just a small piece of leather between me and my horse.

"Sit tall. Chins high. Backs straight." Lauren barked the commands and we responded. "The reins are held loosely in your hands, threaded between your pinkie finger and the one next to it. Elbows in. Very good, class."

I smiled. I had mastered holding the reins. Horseback riding was going to be easy.

"Take a deep breath. And let's walk our horses round the ring again."

We circled the edge of the wooden enclosure, and I muttered to myself under my breath. "Back straight, reins loose, chin up."

42

Suddenly I noticed Lauren was walking beside me. She chuckled at my mumbling and added, "Breathe, Mallory. That's very important. Wouldn't want you keeling over in the middle of the ring."

Some of the other kids laughed at her joke, but I didn't feel embarrassed because Lauren added, "That goes for all of you. Remember, riding is fun. Try to relax and enjoy it."

This time we all laughed. Once again I had a chance to look around me. And that's when I saw him. My dream horse.

He was an Arabian with a beautiful head and delicate nostrils. He was nearly all white, with a white mane and tail and a light dappling of gray that made his coat look like marble. His rider was a somber dark-haired boy with glasses who didn't seem to realize that he was riding the most beautiful horse in the world.

"All right, class," Lauren called, as we circled the ring. "I want you to gently squeeze the sides of your horse with the inside of your boots. We're going to attempt an easy trot. The most important thing to remember about trotting is to keep your heels down and toes up."

"Heels down and toes up," we repeated. "Heels down. Toes up."

"Rise with the motion of the horse, rocking

your pelvis forward and back as the horse trots," Lauren said as we rode past her around the ring. "This is called posting. That'll keep your teeth from banging together, Kelsey," she called to the snooty girl.

I gloated secretly, even though my own teeth were doing a pretty good job of clacking against each other in time to Isabelle's jolting movement. After circling the ring twice I felt that I was getting the hang of trotting. I stole a look out of the corner of my eye at the beautiful Arabian horse behind me. His thick mane was flowing in the breeze, and for a moment I pictured myself in brand-new riding clothes, sitting on his back in front of hundreds of spectators.

"Now, this is the tricky part, class," Lauren called. "I'm going to ask you to reverse directions."

Half of the class started turning their horses before she could give the order to the other half of the class. And for a moment it looked like we were going to have a head-on collision. Lauren waved her crop in the air and bellowed, "Halt!"

We yanked on our reins and managed to pull our horses to a stop. Lauren was laughing. "That was a close one," she cried. "Oh, I wish I had that on tape!"

That made us giggle, and I beamed at my

classmates. I knew I was going to love the next eight weeks.

Lauren explained the proper way to stop a horse, told us how to reverse directions without colliding with the other horses, and suddenly the hour was up.

Then came my favorite part of the whole day: the cool down and grooming. First we walked our horses around the stable yard. Then we uncinched their saddles and after slipping off their blankets, currycombed and brushed their coats until they shone.

I managed to groom Isabelle beside the Arabian. I was certain he belonged to the boy with the glasses. A horse like that was too beautiful just to be part of a stable. It took me a while to get up the courage, but finally I said, "That's a beautiful horse you have. What's his name?"

"Pax." The boy pushed his glasses up on his nose. "But he's not my horse."

"He's not?" My eyes widened. "You mean he belongs to Kendallwood Farm?"

The boy nodded. "All the horses in our class do."

This was great news. That meant that *I* might get to ride Pax at my next lesson. I could hardly contain my excitement.

After class, I hopped on my bike and pedaled as fast as I could to my house. I didn't even stop to take off my coat or say hello to my family but ran right up stairs and headed for the phone. I had to tell Jessi about my fabulous day.

As soon as I heard her soft hello on the other end, I blurted out in a rush, "Jessi, my lesson was wonderful. There are twelve kids in my class and my teacher is Lauren Kendall, and she used to ride on the Olympic riding team, and she is *so* beautiful. Can you believe it?"

"That's great, Mal."

I launched into a breathless description of the lesson, starting with when we were assigned our horses and ending with when we groomed our horses in the stalls. I went over every single detail but one. I left out feeling like a complete dork in my outfit. I didn't want Jessi to think I'd had a bad time.

"And here's the best part," I went on. "I met my dream horse."

"Oh, really?" Jessi sounded a little distracted, but I figured she was helping her mom make lunch or something. So I continued my rave report about Pax.

"He's everything we hoped he'd be, Jessi. A white Arabian with a wonderful personality. You should have seen him trotting around the ring with his head held high. He looked like he was dancing. Oh, you would have loved him!"

I waited for Jessi to respond. When I didn't

hear anything, I asked, "Jessi? Are you still there?"

"I'm here." Her voice sounded distant and cold. I realized something must have happened at home and maybe I had called her at a bad time. I probably would have figured that out right away if I hadn't been so excited about Pax.

"Listen, Jessi, you sound kind of busy," I said.

I thought that would be the perfect opportunity for her to tell me what was wrong. Instead she just said, "Yeah, I really am. I'm sorry, Mal, but I'll talk to you later."

I opened my mouth to say good-bye, but the line clicked off. That was weird. It wasn't like Jessi to be rude. I stared at the receiver, listening to the dial tone. Finally I hung up.

A disturbing thought came to me. Could I somehow have done something to make my best friend angry with me?

# CHAPTER 6

Tuesday

You guys? I think I've got a problem. I sat for the Marshalls today and Nina just wasn't herself. You know how happy and helpful she can be. Well, she just sat in her rocking chair in the living room and stared at the floor. Mrs. Marshall was sort of worried about her. Mal, was she like that when you sat for her last week? I thought I'd talk to you guys before I did anything about Nina.

Jessi's entry in the notebook was pretty weird. If she wanted to know about Nina, why didn't she just call me? I could have talked to her about Blankie. I decided she must have been too busy with her ballet lessons and sitting jobs to call me, and that we'd have time for a good talk after the next BSC meeting.

Anyway, Jessi went to the Marshalls' house on Tuesday afternoon. Mrs. Marshall met her at the front door and kept her on the front porch for a few minutes so they could talk without Nina or Eleanor overhearing them.

"Jessi," Mrs. Marshall said in a hushed voice, "Nina is having some problems at preschool."

"What's the matter?" Jessi asked.

"I'm not sure." Mrs. Marshall pushed a strand of hair off her forehead. "But I received a note from her teacher today saying he thought Nina was uneasy about something, but he wasn't sure what."

"Did the teacher try to talk to Nina about it?"

Mrs. Marshall nodded. "Yes, but she wouldn't open up to him."

Jessi tilted her head. "That's strange. Usually Nina likes to talk."

"I know." Mrs. Marshall sighed. "But she

won't even tell *me* what's wrong. She just mopes around the house."

"Well, I'll see if I can find out anything," Jessi said.

"That would be a great help." Mrs. Marshall started to lead Jessi into the house, then added in a whisper, "In the meantime, don't be surprised if she gets a little teary-eyed about things."

Jessi nodded. "I understand."

While Mrs. Marshall got her coat from the front closet, Jessi peered around the corner into the living room. Eleanor was on the floor in front of the television, happily watching *Sesame Street*. But Nina wasn't even looking at the TV. She was just sitting in her chair off to the side, clutching her huge gray blanket.

"Hi, Nina."

Jessi waved, but Nina looked at her without smiling. When Eleanor noticed Jessi, though, she hopped to her feet, and waddled toward her with her arms open wide.

"Hello, Eleanor." Jessi scooped her up and groaned good-naturedly. "Boy, are you turning into a big girl," she told her.

Mrs. Marshall poked her head into the living room from the hall. " 'Bye-bye, kids. You be good for Jessi and I'll be back in a very short time."

" 'Bye, Mommy." Eleanor put her hand to her mouth and blew kisses at her mother. Jessi noticed that Nina barely mumbled good-bye.

Once the front door had shut, Jessi turned to Nina. "Now it's just the three of us," she declared cheerfully. "What should we play?"

Nina shrugged. "I don't know."

Jessi carried Eleanor into the hall, where she had left her things, and said, "My Kid-Kit has some pretty fun stuff in it today. Maybe we should take a look at it."

This time Nina looked up, but she still didn't budge from her chair. Jessi carried the carton to Nina's side and set it down next to her.

"Here, Nina," Jessi said as she lowered Eleanor to the floor. "Why don't you open it up?"

Nina slid out of her chair onto the rug, pulling her blanket into a huge ball on her lap. She opened the carton listlessly and peered inside. As she rummaged through the box, Jessi noticed that Nina never let go of the blanket at any time. She decided to ask her about Blankie — at the right moment.

That moment came when Eleanor and Nina found a brand-new pack of crayons in the box, and Nina started coloring a paper doll. She relaxed a little. Jessi watched her for a moment, then asked in an offhand way, "Nina, did you take Blankie with you to school today?''

Nina drew back as if she'd been pinched. Finally she mumbled, "Yes.''

"Did you two have a good time?''

Nina didn't answer. She just methodically took the crayons out of their box and placed them on the rug beside the doll she was coloring. Every now and then she would adjust her blanket around her knees, as if reassuring herself that it was still there.

Jessi decided that the old gray blanket was Nina's problem. Maybe the kids at school were teasing her about it. But how could her teacher not notice that? Especially since Nina's blanket was so enormous. Unless the other children teased Nina behind the teacher's back.

Jessi knew all too well how that could happen. When she first moved to Stoneybrook, some of the kids at school and even a few adults were mean to her, just because of the color of her skin. Jessi didn't tell her teachers about it, because she was afraid the kids would think she was a tattletale. Maybe Nina was having the same kind of trouble.

"You know, Nina, when I first moved here, some of the kids at my school weren't very nice to me.'' Jessi took one of the paper dolls out of the box and picked up a crayon. "They teased me and made me feel so bad that I cried."

Nina stopped coloring but didn't look up. "Why?"

"Because they didn't like the way I look."

Nina glanced at Jessi, then reached for another crayon. "I think you look fine."

"Thanks," Jessi said. "But my point is that some of the other kids didn't think so. They were unkind to me just because I was different. But soon they got to know me, and now I have lots of friends."

Jessi studied Nina's face to see if what she was saying had made any sense, but Nina just continued to color. Jessi looked at the doll she was working on and smiled. Talking about skin color as a problem probably *didn't* make sense to a little girl who had just colored her doll's face blue and the hands and legs green.

Jessi gave Nina a quick hug and then went to the kitchen to fix some lemonade. As she filled the girls' plastic animal cups, Jessi wondered if maybe she should tell Mrs. Marshall about Nina's blanket problem and the teasing.

"No," Jessi muttered to herself. "I better wait until I'm sure."

Because what if it wasn't the blanket at all? Then Jessi would have caused a lot of concern for nothing.

I'll talk to the BSC first, Jessi told herself. My friends will know what to do.

The girls drank their lemonades, and after they'd finished, the front doorbell sounded. Jessie waited for Nina to say, "I'll get it," like most kids do, but she just continued to color her doll. Finally Jessi stood up.

"Let's see who it is," she said brightly.

Eleanor, who had been more interested in the outside of the Kid-Kit than in what was in it, hopped to her feet and shouted, "Okay!"

"Come on, Nina." Jessi offered her hand to Nina, who tagged along, dragging her blanket behind her.

What greeted them on the front porch made even Nina laugh. There stood Vanessa, Nicky, Margo, and Claire, wearing red rubber clown noses and polka dot bow ties. Nicky had hung a huge white sign around his neck.

"*Stars of Tomorrow* auditions," Jessi read out loud. "Are you guys looking for more clowns?"

Vanessa shook her head. "We're looking for all kinds of acts for our talent show. And today is your lucky day. We're holding door-to-door auditions."

Jessi laughed. "That sounds like fun. Nina, do you want to audition?"

Nina leaned against Jessi's leg and shook her head.

"Oh, come on," Jessi encouraged her. "I'll bet there are lots of things you can do."

"We need every kind of performer," Vanessa said, checking the clipboard she was carrying. "Singers, dancers, clowns, jugglers, trained dogs, elephants — "

"Hold it a minute," Jessi cut in. "Where are you going to get elephants?"

Claire tugged at Jessi's sleeve. "It's pretend, silly."

Jessi smiled down at Nina. "You could pretend to be an elephant. You could drape yourself in Blankie and stick one arm out for a trunk and you'd look just like an elephant."

Nina considered for a second and then shook her head again. "No, thanks."

"Aw, come on Nina, we're all in the show," Nicky cried. "I'm the strong man wrestling alligators. But I also do acrobatic tricks with Margo. Want to see?"

Jessi checked the sky to see if any rain clouds were lingering overhead and said, "Why don't we sit outside in the backyard and watch them perform their acts?"

Everyone hurried around the side of the house. Vanessa, Nicky, Margo, and Claire conferred quickly to decide who should go first. From the excitement in their voices, Jessi could tell that showing off their talents to the neighborhood was certainly more fun than watching other people audition.

Nina spread her blanket on the grass and let Jessi and Eleanor sit beside her.

Jessi, who loves any kind of a performance (possibly because she spends a lot of time on the stage herself), clapped her hands together and announced, "Curtain going up!"

Nicky did a drumroll with his hands against the side of a trash can while Vanessa stepped in front of the swing set and announced, "And now, *Stars of Tomorrow* presents — Nicholas and Margo doing the Wheelbarrow!"

Nicky walked on his hands while Margo struggled to hold his legs off the grass. They circled the swing set several times as Nina, Eleanor, and Jessi applauded. Then Margo tripped over the garden hose and stumbled forward, shoving Nicky's face into the ground.

"Hey!" Nicky bellowed. "You dented my nose." He sat up and everyone saw that his red clown nose had been smashed flat. Everyone began to laugh. Even Nina.

Then Vanessa took her turn. She walked to the swing set and stood at the foot of the stairs leading up to the slide.

"Ladies and gentlemen," she cried. "I will now climb to the top of this ten-story building," — she clambered up the steps until she was standing on the little platform at the top of the slide — "and perform a death-defying slide to the sidewalk below, using no hands, with my eyes closed."

Nina was very impressed by this announcement. She turned to Jessi and whispered, "Wow."

They watched as Vanessa snapped her fingers at Nicky and ordered, "Drumroll, please."

Nicky beat his hands against the wooden seat of the swing as Vanessa sat down at the top of the slide. She turned to show Jessi and the Marshall kids that her eyes were shut. Then she folded her arms across her chest and began her descent.

Unfortunately, she was wearing shorts, and her bare skin acted like a brake against the metal slide. She hardly moved at all. Vanessa had to scoot bit by bit toward the bottom of the slide. With each jerk her legs made a loud, squeaking sound.

Jessi clutched Nina's hand and whispered, "So much for the death-defying slide. She couldn't go any slower if she tried."

Nina bobbed her head up and down. "She looks like a caterpillar," she giggled.

Vanessa made it gamely to the bottom of the slide and leaped up to take her bow. As the kids cheered and applauded, Jessi thought to herself, "One thing for sure — *Stars of Tomorrow* is going to be the funniest talent show on earth!"

Now it was Claire's turn. Vanessa raised one arm and announced, "*Stars of Tomorrow* proudly presents Miss Claire, the greatest juggler in the world."

Claire raced around the corner of the house. In one hand she held a tennis ball and in the other a Frisbee. Jessi figured Claire must have just found them in the garage. Claire tossed the ball and the Frisbee in the air and tried to catch each object in the opposite hand. Unfortunately the tennis ball bounced off her forehead and rolled into Eleanor's lap, while the Frisbee landed on Claire's own foot.

"Yeow!" Claire cried, clutching her toe with her hands. "Owie-owie-owie!"

Normally Jessi would have gotten up to make sure Claire hadn't hurt herself, but the sight of her in her clown nose hopping up and down on one leg in a circle was so silly that Jessi couldn't help laughing.

Nina clapped her hands and giggled. "She's really funny," she said.

"I bet if you got up there and put on a clown nose," Jessi said, "you could be funny, too."

Nina's laughter stopped instantly. "I don't want to. I'll just watch."

Jessi decided not to push Nina any further. She figured there was still a long time until the talent show. Hopefully Nina's problems at school would be solved by then, and she would change her mind and join the fun.

# CHAPTER 7

My second riding lesson, and I couldn't believe my luck! I got to ride Pax, the beautiful white Arabian. My dream horse. And you know what? He was even more wonderful to ride than to look at.

I arrived at the stables early so that I could talk to Lauren and flat-out ask to ride Pax that day. I also wanted a chance to chat with a few of the other kids in my group before the class started. I figured we'd have lots in common — loving horses, for one thing. But it was strange. None of them seemed to want to talk much.

A short girl with frizzy blonde hair and braces on her teeth was the second to arrive. I marched right up to where she was saddling her mount and said, "My name's Mallory Pike. What's yours?"

She looked kind of surprised that I had spoken to her. "Allison Anders," was all she answered. Then she turned to Lauren and said, "I thought we were required to wear *proper* riding attire for this class."

I felt the tips of my ears turn bright red and my face grow hot.

Lauren must have seen me blush because she said sharply, "Proper riding gear is boots, gloves, and a helmet, Allison. And Mallory is wearing just that." Then her tone softened and she added, "This is a beginner's class. There's no sense in spending a lot of money on gear unless you plan to continue taking lessons."

I wanted to say, "Of course I plan to continue riding. But is it my fault my family can't afford to buy me a fancy habit?" But I didn't. I just took Pax's reins and led him outside.

"Come on, boy," I murmured, nuzzling my head against his neck. "You're a good horse." I shot a dark look back in Allison's direction. "Not a snob like some people I know."

I walked Pax around the stable yard as more and more of my class arrived. The students were all wearing what Allison had called "proper" riding gear. Pax, as if sensing my uneasiness, snorted through his nostrils and gave me a nudge in the side with his nose. I stumbled toward the riding ring. When I looked back at him he gave me another little nudge as if to say, "You're as good as they are. Get in there and let them know that."

I chuckled and nuzzled my face in his neck again. "You're right, Pax. I'm just being silly. All I have to do is talk to them and they'll realize I'm a nice person. Come on."

As I led Pax into the ring, I summoned up my courage and said to a plump girl in front of me, "I just love horses, don't you?"

"Of course," she replied. "I grew up with them. We have eight in our stables."

"You have your own horses?" I was impressed. Then I thought — if she has her own horses, why is she taking beginning riding lessons?

The girl must have guessed from the look on my face what I was thinking. "My parents thought it would be a good idea for someone besides them to give me lessons," she said quickly. "Anyway, I'm just taking classes to learn to ride English style."

"Me, too," I said. "I mean, I already ride Western."

Okay, I'll admit I made it sound like I was pretty good at riding Western style, when all I had done was some trail riding at camp. But I was anxious to make a friend in this class.

"So what's your name?" I asked, casually slipping my foot into the stirrup.

"Megan." She turned a little too suddenly to mount her horse, and he jerked away with a snort. He was already skittish, but she wasn't making him any more relaxed with her sudden movements. Megan gave an impatient yank on the reins and muttered, "Settle down, you dumb horse."

As Megan struggled with her horse, I mounted Pax, who stood perfectly still as I swung onto his saddle. I patted his neck and whispered, "Good horse." Somehow I felt much more confident once I was astride Pax, so I called to Megan, "My name's Mallory. If you like, I'll give you my number and maybe we could get together during the week."

"What?" Megan was still trying to get her horse to stand still. "Oh, sure." She yanked on the reins once more. "Whoa, you idiot."

I did not like the way Megan was talking to her horse, but I figured she probably knew more about horse discipline than I did, since she had eight of her own. Eight. Can you imagine it? One for each day of the week, with one extra for holidays.

Pax and I circled the ring and I paused several times to introduce myself to my classmates. One girl named Kyle even smiled at me. "I like that horse," she said. "I wanted to ride him today."

"He's wonderful, isn't he?" I patted Pax on the neck proudly. "Maybe you can ride him next Saturday." Secretly I was hoping I could ride him every week.

After we chatted about Pax, I told Kyle my name and suggested that maybe we could get together sometime. "We're the only Pike in the Stoneybrook phone book," I said.

Kyle nodded pleasantly and I continued to trot around the ring. I'd made two new friends and I was riding Pax. It was a perfect day!

A few moments later Lauren entered the ring and started class. We reviewed our walking and trotting techniques from the week before. Pax was a dream. He seemed to know what I wanted him to do before *I* even knew it. As the hour went on, I found the courage to wave to several of the students. One boy — the one who had ridden Pax the week before — waved back. I decided he seemed like a nice person, so after class, as we were grooming our horses, I made sure I stood next to him.

"Your name's David, isn't it?" I said as I ran the brush across Pax's broad back. When the boy nodded yes, I continued, "Well, I don't know if I told you last week, but my name's Mallory Pike. I go to Stoneybrook Middle School."

"Oh?"

I took that to mean he was still interested in talking. So for the next five minutes I rattled on nonstop. I told him about my family, my best friend, and the Baby-sitters Club.

"Jessi and I have seen practically every horse movie that was ever made," I said, carefully pulling a few tangles out of Pax's mane. "My friends say I'm horse-crazy. Which is why I wanted to take this class." It suddenly occurred to me that I hadn't let him squeeze a word into the conversation. "So why are you taking this class?"

"My parents made me," he said. "Riding is a tradition in my family."

"But don't you like it?"

He shrugged. "It's okay, I guess."

"Oh, you're kidding, right?" I exclaimed. "I mean, how could you ride a beautiful horse like Pax and not think horses are absolutely wonderful?"

David's face softened as he looked over at Pax. "He is a pretty cool horse." He patted Pax lightly on the neck. The horse craned his head around and nuzzled David's palm.

"That tickles." David laughed and pulled his hand away.

"He's begging for a treat," I explained.

Pax whinnied and then we both laughed.

"How many kids are in your family?" I asked.

"I'm an only child," David replied as he scratched Pax between the ears.

"Hey, maybe you'd like to meet my brothers and sisters. People come over to our house all the time. It's like a big circus. I'll give you my phone number and you could come visit."

I know it sounds like I was being pushy, but David was shy and *needed* a little push. Anyway, I wrote my phone number on a Post-It from the stable office and gave it to David. He put it in his pocket and said, "Thanks." If he didn't want it, he could have given it back, right?

As I rode my bike home that afternoon, I reviewed the new events in my life. I was learning to be a horsewoman. I'd ridden Pax, my dream horse, and I'd taken a stab at making some new friends. Megan seemed okay, Kyle was nice, and David even had my phone number. One of them would probably give me a call before the week was up.

"Hi, Mallory," said my mother as I came in the back door. "Lunch will be ready in ten minutes."

"Great, Mom, I'm starved." I snuck a warm roll from the basket resting on the kitchen counter. "That gives me just enough time to call Jessi."

My mother swatted my hand. "Why can't you wait till the food gets to the table?" She complained.

I laughed and stuffed the whole roll into my mouth. "It tastes better this way," I mumbled.

Then I took the stairs three at a time and

reached for the hall phone. I dialed Jessi without even looking at the numbers.

"Hi," I cried when she picked up. "It's me."

"Hi, Mal. I was just thinking about you." Jessi sounded like her old self. "What are you doing today?"

"Jessi!" I gasped. "What kind of question is that? I just had my second riding lesson. Remember?"

"Oh."

"It's only the most important thing in my life right now," I pointed out.

"I'm sorry, Mal. I guess I forgot."

"Well, aren't you going to ask me how it went?"

There was a long pause. Finally Jessi asked, "How was it?"

"Fantastic. I got there early and Lauren — that's my teacher — let me ride Pax."

"Pax?"

"My dream horse. Don't you remember, Jessi? I told you about him last week."

"Oh, yeah. Right."

Suddenly Jessi didn't sound like herself at all. If I hadn't known her so well, I would have thought she was snubbing me. Even so, I tried to tell her about my new friends.

"There's this boy named David. He's got dark hair and glasses and he's kind of shy — but nice. He rode Pax last week. I think he'll be coming over to visit. You should meet him. And then there's this girl named Megan. Her family owns eight horses and they have their own stables, can you believe it?"

"Really."

Jessi couldn't have cared less about anything I was saying. I was starting to feel uncomfortable.

"Megan will probably be calling me, too — "

"Listen, Mal," Jessi interrupted, "I've got a lot of chores to do today. I'd better not talk on the phone too long. Okay?"

"Oh, well, sure. If you have to go." This was weird. Jessi had never cut me off before. "I just thought you'd like to hear my good news."

"I'd like to, but I don't really have the time. Sorry."

I couldn't help it. My stomach tightened into a hard knot, and suddenly I felt angry. Jessi was supposed to be my best friend and here she was treating me like a stranger.

"Fine." My voice sounded as dead as Jessi's did. "Then maybe I'll see you at school."

I waited for Jessi to say something about getting together over the weekend. Usually we hang out as much as possible. But she didn't even suggest it. Which made me even madder. I set the phone on its hook. Then without thinking I picked it up again and slammed it down hard.

"That's just fine with me," I muttered through clenched teeth. "I don't need your friendship. I can see all my new friends. Like David. And Megan. And Kyle." I picked up the phone again. "I'll show you. I'll just call them." But when I put the phone to my ear, I realized I didn't know David or Megan or Kyle's phone numbers or even their last names. I set the phone down and shrugged. "Oh, well. They'll call me."

A week passed and Jessi and I barely spoke. She went to her ballet lessons, and even though we both had baby-sitting jobs, that didn't explain why we weren't calling each other. And what about all those new friends I'd made at Kendallwood Farm? Well, I didn't hear from a single soul.

# CHAPTER 8

*T hunk.* I hit the ground so hard the wind was knocked out of me. Has that ever happened to you? It's the most terrible feeling in the world.

It was my third lesson at Kendallwood Farm and I wasn't riding Pax. I was riding Gremlin, the horse Megan had struggled with the week before. I should have known I was going to have trouble when he bucked every time I put my foot in the stirrup. Lauren finally held him until I was able to get in the saddle, but the entire lesson went downhill from there.

First of all, Kyle and David, whom I had expected to call me during the week, didn't even say hello to me. You'd have thought we'd never met. Kyle did sort of smile in my direction, but that was it. Then Lauren ran us quickly through our lesson — more walking and trotting and reversing directions. Gremlin kept pushing up against the riding rail. I knew exactly what he was doing. He was trying to scrape me out of the saddle. Normally I would have laughed about it with the rest of the riders in my class, but none of them seemed to be aware that I even existed, let alone that I might be having trouble.

"Okay, everyone, today we're going to learn how to canter," Lauren announced from the center of the ring as we rode around and around her. "The canter cue is an easy one. Simply keep your outside leg where it is, and move your inside leg back about two inches. Then squeeze your horse with your legs."

I was concentrating so much on where my legs were supposed to go that I forgot to keep a firm grip on the reins. When she said, "Squeeze your horse," I did.

Gremlin bolted forward like he'd been jabbed with a needle. He bucked twice and I flipped backwards out of the saddle. I landed flat on my back. Luckily I was wearing my riding helmet because my head bounced hard against the ground. As soon as I hit the dirt, every muscle in my body seemed to lock and I couldn't breathe in or out. For a second I was sure I was going to die. I lay on the ground in a daze, vaguely aware of the pounding horses and their riders struggling to avoid stepping on me.

"Come to a halt, class!" Lauren shouted. "Halt!"

She raced to my side, and it was only when she reached me that I was able to breathe. I sucked in a gulp of air and sat up.

"Mallory, are you all right?"

I turned my head slightly and saw that she was staring hard into my eyes. I think she was checking to see if I had suffered a concussion. The jolt to my body had been so strong and so hard that tears rushed to my eyes and streamed down my cheeks. It was really embarrassing. I couldn't stop the tears. I tried to cover my face with my hands so the rest of the class couldn't see, but I knew they already had. Then my hands started shaking.

"Mallory," I heard Lauren say in a gentle voice. "Do you think you can stand?"

I tried to answer but my mouth wasn't working right. So I just nodded.

"Here, I'll help you walk over to the bench." Lauren pulled me carefully to my feet. My legs felt like rubber. I could barely control them, so I had to lean on Lauren's arm for support.

What a jerk I was. Crying and shaking like that. Worse, the rest of the class just stared at me like I was some strange being from another planet. I saw one girl whisper behind her hands to the girl next to her, who giggled. She stopped quickly when Lauren shot her a hard look.

"Amber?" Lauren barked. "Lead the class in trotting until I get back."

Lauren led me to a wooden bench at the side of the ring and asked me to move my arms and legs to make sure nothing was broken. "Are you sure you're okay, Mallory? You had a pretty bad fall."

I wiped my nose. It had started running (naturally), so besides feeling stupid I also felt ugly. "I think so," I said. "But I'm still a little shaky."

Lauren nodded and stood up. "Just to be on the safe side, I'm going to call your mother and have her come pick you up." She patted me lightly on the shoulder. "I think you've done enough riding for today."

"Thanks," I mumbled, staring at the ground. Normally I would have protested, but I was too woozy to ride my bike home. I felt like a wimp. In the movies, whenever a rider takes a fall, he or she always gets right back on the horse, just to show confidence.

Lauren leaned over and whispered, "Listen, every good rider suffers a fall like this. More than once, I hate to say. So there's no need to feel ashamed." She straightened up and sighed. "Besides, I think it's about time to retire Gremlin. He's been giving everyone trouble."

Her words were intended to reassure me, but they didn't. I still felt embarrassed and hurt and angry. I knew the rest of the kids in my class were thinking I was a klutz. And I was afraid they were right. I closed my eyes, wishing I could just make a wish, and *poof*, I'd be home.

My mom arrived ten minutes later. She leaped out of the car without turning off the engine and ran toward me across the paddock. "Mallory, are you okay? Can you walk?"

I felt a huge wave of relief. I didn't care if the other kids were watching or not. I got up and limped to my mom and let her hug me. I hugged her back hard. "I think I'm fine. I feel shaky and bruised, but Lauren doesn't think anything's broken."

My mother helped me to the car, running around to open the door on my side. "I think we'd better take you to the hospital, just to be sure."

"Oh, Mom," I protested weakly. "I'm okay, really."

"No arguments." My mother hopped into the driver's seat and put the station wagon in drive. "I've already called Dr. Calloway. He and your father will meet us at the emergency room."

On the way to Stoneybrook General Hospital I told Mom about my accident. I exaggerated a little about how mean Gremlin was, and how he bolted when I gave him the canter cue, but I didn't need to elaborate on the description of having my breath knocked out of me. It was vivid in my memory.

My mother listened with a worried frown on her face. She gasped in all the right places and made sympathetic noises when I described how much the fall hurt. It felt good to be able to tell her about it.

Dad met us at the front entrance and helped me into the waiting room. I could tell he was worried about me because he was treating me as if I were a basket of eggs. "Do you want me to carry you inside?" he asked.

"Dad!" I looked around quickly to make sure no cute guys were in hearing distance. "I'm really okay," I reassured him. "Honest."

"That is a dangerous sport," my mom declared while she filled out the insurance papers at the front desk. "You've had a bad fall. We're not leaving here until I'm sure you're all right."

The nurse ushered us into an empty examining room, where we waited for Dr. Calloway to arrive. He'd been out at the golf course, so when he came in he wasn't wearing his usual white coat. Instead he had on these bright yellow pants, an electric blue polo shirt, and a visor.

"Sorry to call you away from your game," Dad said.

Dr. Calloway waved one hand. "It's no problem." He slipped on his stethoscope, found a small pen light, and ran me through a series of tests.

First he listened to my heart. Then he shone the light in my eyes while asking me to look in various directions. Finally he tested my reflexes by tapping my knees with a little rubber hammer. After about ten minutes he looked up at my parents and announced, "Well, I think she'll live."

I giggled and he grinned at me. "There, you see? Laughter *is* the best medicine." Dr. Calloway tucked his stethoscope away and said, "We don't need an X-ray, but you've had a pretty hard fall, young lady. One you probably won't forget."

Boy, was he right about that!

"I'd advise," he continued, "that you take it a little easier next time. Choose a different horse."

"I'm not sure there should be a next time," my mother said as we were riding home in the car.

"I think we should let Mallory be the judge of that," my dad replied. He looked at me in the rearview mirror and raised his eyebrows. "How do you feel about it, Mal? Do you want to quit your lessons? We'd understand if you did."

"No way!" I blurted out.

After all I'd gone through to get a chance to take riding lessons, I wasn't about to let one fall stop me. Besides, if I left the class, I'd never see Pax again. How could I stop seeing my dream horse?

"I want to keep riding," I pleaded. "Please, Mom, I'll be careful."

After a lot of fast talking my mother gave in — but only on the condition that I would never ride Gremlin again.

She didn't have to worry about that. Lauren replaced Gremlin with a bay gelding named Samson. He was really gentle but *huge*. So huge I was afraid to ride him.

But not just Samson. After the accident, I was afraid to ride any horse. Even Pax, the nicest, most gentle horse in the stable. It took all of my self-control just to get on his back. Whenever Lauren would tell us to mount up, I would feel this awful knot in my stomach and a rushing in my head. My legs would ache for hours after each lesson because I was gripping the horse too hard. I could barely concentrate on what Lauren said to us. With every bounce in the saddle, my mind would scream,

Don't fall off! Whatever you do, don't fall off!

Things became worse and worse. I started to dread the end of the school week. Every Friday night, I'd toss and turn and then on Saturday mornings I'd do everything to avoid going to the stables. It didn't help that the rest of the kids in my riding class pretty much ignored me.

Worst of all, there was no one I could talk to about being afraid. Not Mom or Dad. The lessons had cost them too much. So there I was. I had gotten everything I'd said I wanted — riding lessons and my dream horse. And I was totally miserable.

But what I missed most was my friendship with Jessi. A month before, I could have told her how I felt and she would have understood. Now we seemed to be drifting apart, and I didn't know what to do about it.

# CHAPTER
# 9

It was a madhouse at the Pikes' on Saturday. Claud and I had no idea that Vanessa, Nicky, Claire, and Margo could be so goofy.

Come on, Stacey, they're relayted to Mal, arn't they? They have to be Looney Tons.

I'm sure, Mal, that Claudia meant that in the nicest possible way.

I did.

Anyway, Mal was at her riding lesson and we hardly had to do a thing the whole day except—

Watch the intire nayborhood preform.

And laugh.

And laff and laff.

I would have given anything to be able to stay home and watch the kids rehearse their talent show, but I had made a commitment to riding lessons.

Claudia met Stacey, who lives right behind me, on her front porch that morning. Together they walked over to our house and rang the doorbell. It was answered by one of the triplets.

"Hi, Byron," said Claudia.

"Hi," my brother replied, pulling the door back for the girls. "Come on in. You're just in time for the dress rehearsal for the big talent show."

Claudia and Stacey had heard about the show but hadn't had an opportunity to see it yet.

"Are all of you kids in it?" Stacey asked as Byron led them outside.

"Not me. No way," Byron replied. "Just Margo, Nicky, Vanessa, and Claire. They call it *Stars of Tomorrow*."

"Sounds like a big deal," Claudia said.

Byron made a face. "From the way Vanessa is acting you'd think this thing was going to be on national television."

"She's pretty bossy, huh?" Claud laughed.

"You said it," Byron replied. He motioned

toward the door. "They're all out there getting ready."

Stacey and Claud had been hired to sit for all of my brothers and sisters, so Stacey asked, "What are you and Adam and Jordan up to this morning?"

"We're playing Nintendo in the rec room."

"Well, let us know if you decide to go anywhere, or if you need anything," Claudia called over her shoulder as she followed Stacey outside.

"Okay."

Stacey and Claudia stepped into the yard and gasped. Every inch of the yard was crowded with children and pets.

"The entire neighborhood must be here," Claudia said.

Vanessa stood off to the side, shouting through a megaphone that she had made out of poster board. The word "Director" was printed in big letters on the side. "Will the contestants for the *Stars of Tomorrow* talent show please stop talking and lend me your ears?"

"We're supposed to give her our ears?" a little girl in a pink tutu with rabbit ears asked the group in general.

Claudia giggled while Stacey knelt beside the girl and explained, "I think she wants you to sit down and listen to her."

The girl hiked up the front of her leotard. "Then why didn't she say so?"

No one seemed to have heard Vanessa's announcement. The kids continued their excited chatter. Finally Vanessa climbed on a lawn chair and bellowed, "Be quiet and sit down!"

There was a shocked silence as the kids stopped talking and looked around to see who was shouting at them.

"That got their attention," Claudia murmured to Stacey.

The triumphant smile on Vanessa's face vanished as the chair she was standing on slowly folded in the middle and collapsed. She fell backwards onto the grass with a yelp. The kids applauded.

"Way to go, Vanessa!" Nicky shouted.

"Was that your talent?" another one asked.

"Very funny," Vanessa muttered from where she lay sprawled on the grass.

"I better make sure she's okay," Stacey said.

Vanessa was pulling her crumpled megaphone out from under her when Stacey reached her. A grass stain ran down the side of her white tights, but otherwise only her pride had been injured.

"Did that look too stupid?" Vanessa whispered.

Stacey shook her head. "No, you handled it like a pro. But next time, make sure you stand on something sturdy, like a bench."

"Okay." Vanessa leaped up and brushed the grass off her legs. Then she returned to directing the talent contest. "We're going to run through our show, everybody," she called. "I've arranged it in alphabetical order, so Sean Addison — you will go first."

"Where are the other Pikes?" Stacey whispered to Claud.

Claudia stood up. "Margo and Claire are sitting in the front by Vanessa," she reported. "And Nicky is over there talking to Buddy Barrett."

Stacey nodded. "We might as well sit back and enjoy the show."

Stacey and Claud sat on the ground in front of the *Stars of Tomorrow* stage. Well, it wasn't really a stage. It was just a clothesline with two blankets draped across it to look like a curtain. Claud giggled and pointed as Sean Addison punched at the blankets, struggling for a way to get through. Finally he found the opening and emerged in front of the audience. He was carrying a shiny metal tuba that was almost as big as he was. Sean looked over at Margo, who stared back at him blankly. Then Vanessa jabbed her with her elbow and hissed, "You're supposed to introduce him, silly!"

"Oh!" Margo stood up and shouted, "Sean

Addison will be playing a classical song on his tuba."

There was a burst of applause and Sean bowed stiffly, then puffed his cheeks out as he began his song.

Stacey listened for a few seconds, then said, "Hey, that's not a classical tune. That's 'Old MacDonald.'"

Claudia covered her mouth to keep from laughing out loud. "I think she meant a song from their class at school."

Sean played the notes perfectly — all except the last one — so the tune sounded like, "Ee-ai-ee-ai-*YEOW!*" But he didn't seem to notice. He bowed solemnly from the waist and stuck out his tongue at Buddy Barrett, who was next.

Buddy didn't bother to come through the curtains. He was carrying too many props in his arms — a hula hoop, a paper bag, and a large red ball. His younger sister Suzi waddled after him, tugging on a leash. At its end was their basset hound, Pow.

"Don't worry, I'll introduce us," Buddy said to Vanessa. Then he stepped forward and gestured with his thumb to his chest. "I am Buddy Barrett, the world's greatest animal trainer."

"Since when does an animal trainer wear a Cub Scout uniform?" Stacey whispered to Claudia.

"When he can't find anything else to wear," Claudia murmured back.

"And now I'd like to present Pow, the smartest dog on earth," Buddy continued, gesturing grandly to the side. "Bring Pow forward, oh, assistant of mine."

" 'Oh, assistant of mine'?" Claudia repeated. She would have burst out laughing if Stacey hadn't jabbed her in the side with her elbow.

Suzi Barrett led the basset hound out to the center of the stage. He sat on his haunches, his long ears dragging on the ground by his front paws, and stared impassively at the crowd while Buddy declared, "This is Pow, the world's only talking dog."

"This I gotta see," said Claudia, giggling. She leaned forward.

Buddy knelt beside Pow and lifted one of his ears. "All right, Pow, here's your first question. What's on top of the house?"

Buddy and the kids stared hard at the wrinkled basset hound. But Pow did nothing. Buddy repeated the question. This time Pow blinked several times and lazily scratched a flea behind his ear with his back leg. Finally Buddy stood up and shouted, "*SPEAK* to me, Pow."

Pow promptly cocked his head and let out a loud, "Woof."

"That is correct!" Buddy handed the dog a biscuit, which Pow seemed to inhale without chewing. "A roof is on top of the house. See how smart he is, folks?"

The kids giggled and then a boy shouted, "Ask him another question. I'll bet he gives the same answer."

"That's what you think." Buddy grinned at the boy, then turned to Pow and asked, "Okay, how was your day?"

This time Buddy gently nudged Pow in the rear with the toe of his shoe and Pow grumbled, "R-r-r-ruff."

Buddy raised his arms in triumph. "You heard him say it. Pow had a *rough* day."

There was a burst of applause. Then a girl dressed like a radish yelled, "What's the hula hoop for?"

Buddy frowned at her. "I'm getting to that." He turned to Suzi and said, "Assistant, may I have the hoop?"

Suzi ran forward and knelt on the grass, holding the hoop in front of Pow. Pow, however, had decided to lie down, his big head resting on his paws and his ears spread out across the grass on either side.

"I hope this next trick doesn't take too much energy," Stacey whispered to Claudia. "It looks like Pow's falling asleep."

"Pow, the mighty basset hound, will now jump through the hoop." Buddy placed a dog biscuit on the other side of the hoop and clapped his hands. "Okay, Pow — go for it!"

After several moments of intense urging, accompanied by lots of giggling from the neighborhood kids, Pow struggled to his feet. He strolled over to the hoop, stuck his head through it, and inhaled the biscuit. Then he sauntered to the shady side of the house and, with a tired groan, lay down again.

"I think Pow is letting us know your act is over," Vanessa informed Buddy.

Buddy put his hands on his hips and marched over to the sidelines to give Pow a stern lecture about leaving the stage too soon. In the meantime Vanessa checked her clipboard to see who was on next.

Stacey surveyed the crowd. "If they're going in alphabetical order, it should be Haley Braddock's turn next."

They watched as Haley marched briskly through the crowd up to the stage. She wore sequined red shorts, a white sailor blouse, a bow tie also covered with sequins, and a top hat. Stacey saw the baton in Haley's hand and said, "I didn't know she was a twirler."

Haley handed Vanessa a tape recorder, then strode to the center of the stage and lowered herself into a split. She waited for the taped music to begin, a wide smile frozen on her face. But nothing happened.

Claudia and Stacey heard her mumble, "Start the music." But Vanessa didn't hear her. She was too busy trying to keep Charlotte Johanssen's schnauzer Carrot away from another little girl's cat.

Finally, just as Haley was standing up to see what was the matter, Vanessa gasped, "Oh, the music!" She hit the button and "You're a Grand Old Flag" blared out of the recorder, but Haley was no longer in a split.

"Wait!" she yelped. "I'm not ready!"

While the two girls hurried to reset the tape player, Claudia spotted a familiar figure in the Pikes' driveway. "Hey, look, it's Mary Anne." She gestured for her to join them.

Stacey squinted at the house. "She brought Nina Marshall with her. And Nina brought her blanket."

"Oops!" Claudia and Stacey murmured simultaneously as they watched the huge blanket get caught on the fender of a car. Nina pulled it free, but Carrot the schnauzer pounced on the tip dragging behind her. He grabbed it with his teeth and tugged it back and forth with a growl.

"My Blankie!" Nina wailed. "Let go!"

"It's a tug-of-war!" Claudia said. Mary Anne

tried to catch Carrot, but he was too quick for her. "Come on," Claud said, leaping to her feet.

Claud flung herself at Carrot and held on tightly while Stacey pulled the frayed blanket out of Carrot's mouth. Aside from a few dangling threads, there was no damage. Mary Anne gave Nina a quick hug and said, "There. Blankie's okay."

The tears in Nina's eyes dried quickly as the music for Haley's baton twirling number began again. "I want to watch the show!" she cried.

"All right." Mary Anne gathered the gray blanket into a big ball and handed it back to Nina. "But be sure and keep your blanket off the ground. There are a few more dogs around here who might think it's a toy."

Nina clutched Blankie to her chest as she made her way to the second row. Mary Anne waited until Nina was sitting safely on the grass, then sat down with Stacey and Claud and exclaimed, "Phew! That was a close one. Carrot could have ripped that blanket to shreds."

Stacey nodded. "I know. It's old enough."

"Just getting that blanket here in one piece has been a major event. First Nina practically dragged it through a mud puddle. Then we decided to put it in the wagon and pull it, but it's so huge that it caught in the wheel and got all tangled up."

Claud tucked a strand of her long dark hair behind one ear. "That blanket is a major problem," she observed. "It makes it difficult to do anything and keeps Nina from playing with other kids."

"I know." Mary Anne pursed her lips. "But I'm not sure what to do about it."

Stacey shrugged. "Maybe she'll grow out of it."

"I hope so," Mary Anne murmured as she watched several children scoot away from Nina to make way for the blanket. "I really hope so."

# CHAPTER 10

"Mallory, relax," Lauren said to me during my next lesson. "You're stiff as an ironing board."

I couldn't help it. The horse I was riding, whose name was Twilight, had been skittish the entire hour. The first time I gave him the canter cue, he bucked forward just like Gremlin had, and I nearly fell off again. It was all I could do to stay on the horse and complete the lesson.

"All right, class," Lauren called out, raising her arm above her head. "Come to a halt."

Even stopping Twilight was difficult. In my head I went over the command Lauren had taught us. "Sit solidly in the saddle and give a long, firm tug on the reins." I did just that but Twilight ignored me. The rest of the class had reined in their mounts and watched as Twilight and I made one more circle of the ring. As he trotted past Lauren, she reached out and grabbed his bridle.

"Twilight! Whoa!"

The firm tone of her voice stopped him in his tracks. But I wasn't ready for it and pitched forward over his neck. Luckily, I caught his mane and stopped myself from tumbling onto the ground.

"Interesting riding technique," Kelsey murmured as I struggled to sit up straight.

Lauren led me to my position in the circle of riders and whispered in Twilight's ear, "Now you stand there and pay attention."

For the first time that hour, Twilight did exactly as he was told. I couldn't bear to look around because I was sure the rest of the class was laughing at me, so I kept my eyes glued on Lauren, who turned to face the line of riders.

"Class, we have two more lessons left," she announced. "And then this course will be over."

A few murmurs of regret came from the other six kids. But I was relieved, although I wasn't about to admit it in front of Lauren or the class.

Lauren held up her finger. "At the end of each eight-week period, Kendallwood Farm sponsors a horse show and every class participates. You'll all get to show off what you've learned over the past two months."

"Oh, no," I groaned under my breath.

"Our show will be the Sunday after the last class," Lauren continued. "Mark it on your calendars and be sure and tell your family and friends. We'll hand out ribbons to the best riders, so I'd advise you to use the last two lessons to sharpen your skills."

While the rest of the class talked excitedly about who they intended to invite, my mind raced in an entirely different direction. I was trying to come up with an excuse for not being in the horse show. Breaking a leg was out. Too painful. Trying to get the measles probably wouldn't work, either. At any rate, *no way* was I going to invite my family or my friends.

While these thoughts were running through my brain, Amber raised her hand. "Lauren, I'd like to make an announcement, please."

"Go ahead." Lauren gestured for Amber to take the center.

Amber nudged her horse forward. "This Wednesday is my birthday," she announced, "and I would like to invite everyone to come to my party. It should be really cool. I've thought of some fun stuff to do, plus there will be lots of great food. I hope you can all come."

Amber happened to catch my eye and she

smiled. Suddenly I felt a hundred percent better, as if the last hour never happened. Amber had invited *me* to her birthday party. Maybe she liked me after all. I was sure she had smiled specifically at me when she said the words, "I hope you can all come."

Lauren instructed us to dismount, and as we led our horses back to their stalls, I murmured happily to Megan, "Amber's birthday party sounds like lots of fun."

Megan, who had been acting like I didn't even exist, actually grinned. "Amber's parties are always fun."

"Oh, you've been to them before?"

"Sure. Most of the class has. A lot of us go to the same school."

This was news to me, but it explained a lot of things. The other kids already knew each other, which was why I felt like such an outsider. But now that seemed to be changing. I hummed as I currycombed Twilight. I even gave him one of the sugar lumps I had brought for Pax.

"You're not such a bad horse after all, are you, Twilight?" I said.

Twilight stomped his foot as if in reply, and I laughed out loud. Something I hadn't done much of since my second lesson.

I spent the next four days trying to choose the perfect outfit to wear to Amber's party. At first I thought I'd go wild, like Claudia, with tie-dyed tights and a bright purple oversized T-shirt knotted at the bottom, and maybe a big red belt. But then I decided that since I didn't know the kids well I really should dress more conservatively.

Finally Wednesday arrived. My mom picked me up right after the BSC meeting and drove me straight to Amber's. I didn't want to be late. Her house, halfway between Stoneybrook and Stamford, was a huge old colonial with white marble pillars lining the porch and a big circular drive leading to the front door. Music was blasting out of the backyard as we pulled to a stop.

I checked my hair in the mirror one last time and then turned to my mom. "How do I look?"

I was wearing a gold-and-brown kilt, a matching gold cotton sweater, and penny loafers. Mom smiled reassuringly. "You look terrific."

Boy, was she wrong. The second I stepped through Amber's front door I realized I had made a big mistake. First of all, most of the girls were wearing wacky bright clothes with spiked hair and tons of fun jewelry. The guys looked just as cool. I felt as if I were dressed for Sunday school.

I spun around and tried to catch my mom's

attention before she drove away. Too late. The car was just pulling onto the road. My spirits sank as I watched it disappear around the curve. She had promised to pick me up in two hours — so that meant I was just going to have to grin and bear it.

Oh, well, I told myself as I poured a glass of punch at a big oak table covered with sandwiches and pizza. They already think I'm weird because of the way I dress in class. Why confuse them now?

I took my punch, slid a sandwich onto a paper plate, and headed out to the patio. It was decorated with pink lanterns and bunches of neon pink balloons. Two large-screen televisions had been set up at either end and were tuned to MTV. The patio was crammed with dancing kids.

Amber waved at me from the middle of the dance floor. She was wearing a pink-and-black-striped silk top over a pair of hot pink stirrup tights. I hurried to join her.

"Hi, Valerie," she shouted over the music. "I'm glad you could come."

"Um." I cleared my throat. "My name's Mallory, actually."

"Oops." Amber covered her mouth and giggled. "I'm so terrible with names. Have you met my friends?"

"Not yet," I admitted. I was hoping she

meant to take me around and introduce me to them. But Amber waved her hand toward the pool, where another group of kids were tossing a volleyball back and forth over the water. "Just introduce yourself. They're all really great."

"Oh. Thanks, Amber."

The next two hours were agony. I didn't know what else to do, so I edged through the crowd toward the pool. I made a couple of attempts to talk to people, but every time I'd open my mouth to say hello they'd spot one of their friends and disappear. Finally I went back inside.

I spent most of the time hovering around the food table, not because I was hungry but because it gave me something to do. I must have drunk more than ten glasses of punch and eaten half a dozen sandwiches. I bet I strolled out onto the front porch at least fifteen times to see if my mother had come for me early. But no such luck. She was ten minutes late.

"Listen to that music," my mom said as I hopped into the car. "It sounds like the party is still going strong. And since it's a special night, do you want to stay a little longer?"

"*No!*" I practically shouted in her ear. She gave me a startled look and I said quickly, "My stomach feels a little queasy."

"Oh." A knowing smile crossed her face. "Too much cake?"

"And punch." I didn't want to tell her about the party. I was afraid she might say things like, "Well, did *you* introduce yourself? You can't wait for someone else to do it for you, you know." Or, "You should have asked some boy to dance. That would have been a sure way to make friends."

I decided to talk to Jessi about it. I figured she was the only person I knew who'd understand how I felt. I counted the minutes until we got home.

"Jessi, I have to talk to you," I blurted out the second she answered the phone. "The worst thing just happened to me."

"What's the matter, Mal? Is your family okay?" Jessi sounded like her old self, concerned and caring.

"My family's fine. It's me. I went to this party, and it was just terrible."

There was a long pause. Finally Jessi said, "The worst thing that happened is that you went to a terrible party?"

"I know it sounds stupid. But Amber invited me to her birthday party."

"Who's Amber?

"She's from my riding class. I'm sure I mentioned her before."

"A girl from your riding class invited you to her party," Jessi said slowly.

"Yes, and it was awful. There must have been fifty kids there. They had these monster video screens, and lots of dancing, and a swimming pool, and a huge table covered with plates of sandwiches and pizza — "

"Sounds terrible," Jessi said drily.

"No, the party was just fine. The trouble was, I didn't know anyone and — "

"Did you introduce yourself?" Jessi cut in, saying exactly what I would have expected my mom to say.

"I tried, but no one wanted to talk to me. Instead I wound up drinking gallons of punch and feeling stupid."

"Gee, that's too bad."

Jessi didn't sound sympathetic at all. And I felt really silly calling to complain about a party she hadn't been invited to. But it wasn't just the party I wanted to talk to her about. It was every-thing — my rotten riding lessons, my fear of horses, and worst of all, the strained conversa-tions she and I'd been having recently. I just couldn't seem to find the right words.

After a few moments of awful silence, I fi-nally mumbled, "Listen, Jessi, maybe I had too much punch or something. I think I need to lie down."

"Okay."

"I'll see you at school tomorrow."

"Okay."

I went to bed as soon as I hung up the phone, but I barely slept. My dreams were full of strange people in riding boots eating mouthfuls of cake, and big angry horses chasing me around swimming pools filled with punch.

# CHAPTER 11

$M$y final lesson had been scheduled for Thursday afternoon. I guess the party hadn't been so bad after all because the kids in my class seemed a little friendlier to me. Amber's birthday party gave us something to talk about. The kids would say things like, "Wasn't Amber's party a blast?" and I would answer, "It was terrific!" But I still didn't feel part of the group. Maybe because I still hadn't gotten the right clothes. Or maybe because deep down I knew I wasn't comfortable around horses anymore. Would I always be afraid of them?

Anyway, as I said, it was my final lesson. I should have been celebrating, but I just couldn't. Why? Because I still had to go through the horse show the following Sunday. Worst of all, my whole family and the entire membership of the BSC were planning to come to see it.

I had tried to keep quiet about the show, but Kendallwood Farm sent out little notices to our parents. Then my mom told Stacey's mom, and she told Stacey, and that was it. I was stuck.

Now all I could think about was the prospect of making a total fool of myself in front of everybody.

"Mal, you'll be riding Duke today," Lauren called as I entered the stable that morning. My heart dropped into the pit of my stomach.

"Who's riding Pax?" I asked. Even though I had ridden Pax just three times, he was the only horse I felt comfortable with.

"Amber requested him."

I reached for Duke's bridle and reluctantly started to head toward his stall. During the course of our lessons we had been taught to bridle and saddle our horses by ourselves. By now it was such a familiar routine that I hardly thought about it.

I shoved my left hand into the pocket of my jean jacket and felt the carrot I'd brought as a horse treat. I had put sugar cubes in the other pocket. I'd give the sugar to Duke but the carrot was reserved for Pax. Even if I wasn't going to ride him I could at least say hello and give him a treat.

Pax saw me coming and stuck his big beautiful head over his stall door.

"Hi, Pax," I whispered.

He whinnied softly as I rubbed his velvety nose. The warm, moist air from his nostrils tickled the palm of my hand. After I had petted him for a few seconds he snorted and nudged the pocket of my jacket.

"Oh, you clever boy. You knew I brought you a snack." I took a step backwards. "Well, maybe I won't give it to you today," I teased him.

Pax tossed his head impatiently and pawed at the ground.

"Okay, okay, don't be such a baby." I giggled, then pulled out the prized carrot and held it toward him. He devoured it in two bites. "Hey. Slow down." Pax blinked his big brown eyes at me innocently and with a loud crunch finished the last bit of carrot.

As soon as he'd swallowed, Pax nudged my other pocket, where the sugar cubes were. I shook my head.

"Sorry, fella. I have to give those to Duke. That's to make sure he'll be nice to me today."

Pax seemed to understand and pressed his soft muzzle against my cheek. I wrapped my arms around his neck and gave him a strong hug.

"Boy, I wish I were riding you in the show," I mumbled into his mane. "Then maybe I wouldn't be so scared."

By now most of the others in the class had arrived, and I had to hurry to get Duke's bridle and saddle on. Putting on the bridle is my least favorite thing. First of all, you have to stick your finger in the side of the horse's mouth to get him to take the bit. Then you have to pull the leather part over his ears — which most horses hate — and finally you fasten it under his chin.

Duke was pretty good about it today. He especially liked the sugar cube I gave him as a reward. Next I put on his saddle blanket and saddle. This part can get tricky because many horses will hold their breath when you cinch the saddle under their belly. That way, when they exhale, the saddle fits loosely, which is more comfortable for them, but a disaster for the rider. After a couple of trots around the ring, the saddle slips sideways and you find yourself lying on the ground.

After I saddled Duke, I led him to the ring and joined the rest of the kids, who were already astride their horses. This was the part I really dreaded — getting on the horse's back. There was no turning back after that. I took a deep breath, then muttered, "Here goes nothing."

I slipped the toe of my boot into the stirrup and, after several hops, managed to swing my leg over Duke's back. Then I grasped the reins and guided Duke out of the stable into the ring.

Amber was the last to join us. She and Pax trotted into the ring and took their position between Kelsey and Allison. Lauren, who had been standing patiently in the center of the ring, clapped her hands together and smiled at the class. "Well, folks, this is our final lesson. Next week is the horse show, where we find out if anything I've taught you has sunk in."

A couple of kids giggled and Lauren winked at them. "I'm really proud of all of you, and I know that next week you'll do splendidly."

I wished I felt as confident as Lauren sounded. She clapped her hands together. "So. Our plan for today is to go through the exercises just as you will be doing them at the show."

She instructed us to walk our horses in a circle around the ring. That was easy enough. Duke fell in line behind Kelsey, who was riding Twilight, without any protest, and I breathed a little easier. So far, so good.

"Heads held high, backs straight, elbows in, toes up, heels down," Lauren reminded us. "Good. All right, class. Reverse directions and trot. Be sure to change your diagonal."

"Diagonals," I said glumly. They were very confusing. You have to sit for a beat when you change directions.

"Smooth post, class," Lauren barked. "Some of you look like a watermelon bouncing around in your saddle."

I was so busy worrying about my diagonal that I completely forgot about posture or style.

"Reverse directions and canter."

Cantering was the last gait we had learned to do. It was the easiest one, besides walking. You simply sat in the saddle and let your pelvis rock back and forth as if you were riding a rocking horse while the horse did an easy gallop around the ring. The hard part was making sure your horse took the right lead — which meant starting the canter with the correct foot. Luckily, Duke did take the right lead and I started to feel a little more confident.

The final exercise of the day was to keep our horses standing perfectly still. Sounds easy, doesn't it? Well, it was a disaster. I think Duke was all pumped up from getting to run and still wanted to canter. He skipped sideways, knocking into Allison's horse. Then he tried to get out of the line we'd formed by backing up.

"Mallory, be firm," Lauren instructed. "You, too, Kelsey."

I stole a glance at Kelsey and saw that she

was having more trouble than me, trying to keep Twilight under control.

"Now remember," Lauren said, "the judges will come down the line to check how well you carry yourself, and after that it will all be over."

Several of the students let out moans of disappointment, but not me. As it was, it seemed like the horse show was going to be endless.

If I can just make it through without falling off, I told myself, I'll be happy.

"Miss Kendall?" David raised his hand. "What horses will we be riding in the show?"

Lauren snapped her fingers. "I almost forgot. Thank you for reminding me, David." She took off her hunt cap and, taking several pieces of paper from her pocket, placed them inside. "We're going to draw lots. I've numbered these slips from one through six. Whoever pulls out number one chooses first." As she shook the hat, Lauren added, "But remember, in next week's horse show, the judges will only judge the rider — not the horse. That way no one will have an advantage."

Lauren walked around the ring, and each of us reached into the hat and drew out a piece of paper. I was afraid to open mine. I squeezed my eyes shut and whispered, "Please, oh, please, let mine be number one."

But before I even opened my paper, Kelsey

squealed, "I get to pick first. I got number one."

My heart sank. Of course Kelsey would pick Pax. He was the perfect horse. But to my surprise she chose a chestnut named Brandy.

"Who has number two?" Lauren asked, looking around the ring. No one said anything, and I realized I hadn't checked my own number. I unfolded it and gasped in surprise.

"That's me," I said, waving the little piece of paper over my head. "And I choose" — I turned and smiled at the beautiful white horse — "Pax."

I didn't even pay attention to which horses the rest of the class chose. I was too giddy with happiness. For one last time, Pax would be all mine. And right when I really needed him. Just in time for the horse show. Things weren't so bleak after all.

# CHAPTER 12

Thursday

The most terrible, awful thing happened at the Marshalls' today. Who would have thought just washing and drying an old blanket could have such disastrous results? Luckily, it wasn't my idea to wash Nina's blanket. It was Mrs. Marshall's. I guess once a month she manages to pry the thing out of Nina's fingers and clean it. But even then, Nina refuses to leave Blankie's side. When I reached the Marshalls' house, she was sitting in front of the dryer, staring at it like she had x-ray vision and could see inside. Mrs. Marshall gave me a few instructions and left. Twenty minutes later, disaster struck.

Dawn's Disaster happened the following Thursday afternoon. I had bicycled out to Kendallwood Farm to give Pax a carrot and to try to relax my nerves about the horse show. It didn't help much. Pax was as sweet as ever, but I was still tense. The least little noise would make me jump. It's a good thing I wasn't the one baby-sitting for Nina. I probably would have cried louder than she had. Anyway, I think Dawn handled the situation perfectly.

What happened was this. While Nina was in the laundry room staring at the dryer, Mrs. Marshall took Dawn aside and gave her some last-minute instructions.

"The kids can each have yogurt and a graham cracker in about half an hour," she said. "By that time, Blankie should be done. Just pull it out, give it a quick shake — "

"And hand it to Nina," Dawn finished for her.

Mrs. Marshall smiled. "She'll probably take it from you." She shook her head, making a little clucking noise. "Nina attached herself to that blanket almost the moment she was born. She's never been without it."

"Has she ever lost it?" Dawn asked.

"One Christmas we left it at a relative's house and didn't discover it until two hours later. We had to turn the car around immediately and drive back to get it. Nina was practically in hysterics."

Dawn whistled softly between her teeth. "Wow."

"Wow is right." Mrs. Marshall heaved a sigh of frustration. "That blanket has been a big problem. I'm just glad Eleanor isn't obsessed with a blanket or toy."

Mrs. Marshall kissed Eleanor, who was playing with several pots and pans on the kitchen floor, and then called good-bye to Nina. After Mrs. Marshall had gone, Dawn joined Eleanor, who had set one of the saucepans on her head.

"That makes a beautiful hat," Dawn told her.

Eleanor toddled over to the stove, where she peered at her reflection in the glass of the oven door. "Pretty!" she exclaimed.

"Nina, come look at your sister's new hat," Dawn called.

"I can't," Nina replied. "I'm with Blankie. Tell her to come here."

Dawn led Eleanor into the laundry room. Nina was still seated on a step stool, while the dryer went around and around.

"Look at Eleanor's hat," Dawn said.

Eleanor waved the pan proudly in the air and then banged it twice against the side of the washer. Luckily Dawn pulled it out of

Eleanor's hand before she could do any damage to the paint. Eleanor hardly noticed the pan was gone. She continued to bang on the washer with her bare hand.

Nina covered her ears to shut out the loud, hollow sound but continued staring at the dryer.

"That's concentration," Dawn murmured.

Eleanor stopped pounding on the washer and abruptly declared, "Eat. Let's eat."

Dawn checked her watch. Nearly fifteen minutes had passed since Mrs. Marshall had left the house. She figured it would be okay to give the girls their snack a few minutes early. "All right, Eleanor. It's time for yogurt and graham crackers."

"Yea!" Eleanor followed Dawn to the kitchen.

Dawn lifted Eleanor into her high chair and, taking a carton of blueberry yogurt out of the refrigerator, divided it neatly onto two plates.

Eleanor beat her spoon against the plastic tray.

"Here you go," Dawn said, patting her on the head. "And some grahams."

The buzzer sounded from the laundry room, and Nina bellowed, "Blankie is done! Let him out, Dawn. Please let him out."

The way Nina talked, it sounded like Blankie had been locked inside a little cage.

"He's all by himself," she continued. "He wants to get out. Hurry, Dawn!"

"Just a minute," Dawn said, setting the yogurt on Eleanor's tray and the box of graham crackers next to it. Then she ran to the laundry room, where Nina was jumping up and down.

"Careful," Dawn cautioned as she opened the door to the dryer. "Don't put your hand inside, Nina. This is very hot."

"I won't. Just take Blankie out."

Dawn bent down and peered inside the dryer. She couldn't find the thin gray blanket at first. It was plastered against the side of the round drum. She reached gingerly for a corner of it, trying not to touch the hot metal. "Got it," she said as she felt her fingers close around the soft material.

"Give him to me," Nina cried. "Please!"

A harsh tearing sound echoed inside the dryer.

"Oh, my gosh!" Dawn gasped. She held up a ragged scrap of gray material. It had separated from the rest of the blanket.

"My Blankieeee!" Nina's howl could be heard two houses away. "You killed him." She snatched the square of material away from Dawn and plunged her hand inside the hot dryer. Then she howled in pain.

Dawn was shocked by what Nina had done, but it took her only a second to spring into action. She scooped Nina up in her arms and carried her into the kitchen, where she turned on the cold-water faucet. "Hold your hand under there," she told Nina. "It will make the burn feel better." Dawn was relieved to see that Nina had burned only a fingertip.

Still, tears were pouring down Nina's cheeks. Dawn didn't know if it was because of her finger or because of Blankie. Nina let her know almost instantly.

"Blankie!" she wailed. "I want my Blankie."

Until then, Eleanor had been eating contentedly in her high chair. Now her own chin began to quiver.

"It's all right, Eleanor," Dawn reassured her. "Your sister burned her finger. But it will be all better in a second."

"It's not my finger." Nina pulled her hand out from under the faucet and stumbled back toward the laundry room. "I want my Blankie. Please give him to me."

"Nina, I'll get him for you." Dawn ran ahead of her. "Sit on the stool and I'll hand him to you."

Dawn reached into the dryer once more but when she touched the material, the same thing happened again. Blankie pulled apart like cotton candy. "This is a disaster," she said to herself.

Nina saw the next torn piece of blanket and

let out a scream louder than the first one.

"I'm so sorry, Nina." Dawn reached out to comfort her, but Nina pounded her shoulder with her fists.

"You did it," she wailed. "You killed Blankie."

Dawn stood up. Her mind was racing. She turned back to the dryer, pulled out another square of material, and cried, "Look! This Blankie is the perfect size to fit in your pocket." She leaned forward and stuffed it into the pocket of Nina's T-shirt. Before Nina could say anything, Dawn grabbed another torn square. "And this little Blankie will fit into your purse."

Nina stopped wailing and wiped the back of her hand across her nose. Tears continued to stream down her cheeks, but she was intrigued by what Dawn was doing.

"This Blankie is just right to tuck up your sleeve," Dawn continued cheerfully.

Nina giggled through her hiccups. Dawn found another piece of the shredded blanket and tucked it into Nina's shoe.

"Oh, look, he wants to go for a walk. And this one wants to hide in your back pocket."

The tears dried on Nina's cheeks as she began to enjoy the new game Dawn had invented. By the time Dawn was through fishing out the remains of Blankie from the dryer, he was hidden all over Nina. This gave Dawn another great idea.

"Hey!" she exclaimed. "Now you can carry Blankie everywhere you go, and nobody will ever know. He's hidden. In fact, you can keep Blankie all over the place — a piece in your room, a piece in your cubby at school, a piece in your pocket — and he'll be your secret."

"He's really hidden?" Nina looked up at Dawn and blinked her eyes.

"Come with me and I'll show you." Dawn led Nina to the kitchen, where she scooped Eleanor out of her high chair. Then the three of them stood in front of the full-length mirror in the hall. Dawn pointed to Nina's shirt pocket. "See, we know he's hiding in there but no one else will."

Nina giggled and lifted her foot. "I know Blankie's in my shoe, too, but it's *my* secret."

"That's right." Dawn knelt beside Nina and hugged her close. "He'll always be with you," she whispered, "and no one will know."

# CHAPTER 13

It was Friday — forty-eight hours until D-Day (Dying-of-Embarrassment Day). School had been a blur all week. I could think about nothing but the horse show. I was late for classes and missed answers on tests that I should have known. I even forgot about the BSC meeting. Luckily, at five-fifteen my mother stuck her head in my room to remind me. I hopped on my bike and pedaled as fast as I could to Claudia's.

When I arrived, Dawn was telling everyone about the Blankie disaster. I caught most of it — how the blanket had disintegrated in the dryer, and how Dawn had saved the day by stuffing little bits of it into Nina's pockets. Dawn was such a good storyteller that even when Claud's digital clock read 5:30, Kristy didn't interrupt to call the meeting to order. Dawn finished her story and we just stared at her, shaking our heads in amazement.

"Boy, Dawn," Claud said, dropping a handful of potato chips into her mouth. "You really were thinking fast."

"I had to," Dawn said. "Nina was about to have a major tantrum. I'm not kidding. She screamed so loudly that when I was leaving later that afternoon, one of the neighbors asked me if there had been an accident at the Marshall house."

"That must have been embarrassing," Jessi said.

"It was. But — " Dawn held up her crossed fingers and grinned. "Hopefully it will be worth it."

"If you ask me," Stacey said, "I think Nina will have a much easier time at school from now on."

"We'll all have a much easier time," Mary Anne agreed. "I hate to admit it, but the last time I sat for Eleanor and Nina and Blankie, it wasn't much fun."

Kristy cleared her throat and adjusted her visor. "Then I would like to take this opportunity to congratulate Dawn on a job well done. And to say that this meeting of the BSC is officially called to order."

As if in response to Kristy's words, the phone rang. Claud picked up the receiver and said, "Hello, Baby-sitters Club. There's no problem we can't solve."

Stacey snorted with laughter. "She makes us sound like a bunch of detectives."

"Well, in a way we are," Kristy said as Claud scribbled down the caller's information on a pad. "A detective has to be quick on her feet, ready to handle any new situation that comes along, and able to deal with it in a levelheaded way. That's what we do."

Mary Anne cocked her head. "You know, Kristy's right. Dawn solved the Nina-and-Blankie problem. And remember when Mallory figured out what was bothering the Arnold twins?"

I smiled, remembering how I'd discovered that the twins hated being treated like little identical dolls. Once I found that out, they were easy to deal with. I turned to Jessi and said, "What about when Jessi learned sign language so she could talk to Matt Braddock, and then all of the kids in the neighborhood wanted to know Matt's secret language?"

Jessi answered by signing, "Thanks for remembering that."

"Hey!" Claudia dipped her hand into the potato chips again. "Let me know when you're finished congratulating yourselves, so Mary Anne can assign this job."

Everyone laughed and then we got down to business. Friday was busy and the phone rang nonstop. All of the activity almost made me forget about the horse show on Sunday. Almost. Unfortunately, giant butterflies were still flip-flopping around my stomach.

Mary Anne took a job with the Prezziosos, Kristy agreed to three afternoons with the Barretts, and I accepted a job with the Rodowskys. Then Mrs. Marshall called.

Dawn had picked up the phone, and when we heard her say "Oh, hi, Mrs. Marshall," we fell silent. The Blankie idea had worked great on Thursday, but Dawn hadn't heard whether things were still okay. After Mrs. Marshall gave Dawn the details for the next job, Dawn asked, "So how was Nina's day at school?"

"Wonderful!" Mrs. Marshall replied so loudly that we could all hear her. "She came home grinning from ear to ear. And she didn't seem to mind at all that she could only take a piece of Blankie to school."

"That's great," Dawn replied. "Tell her I said hello."

Dawn hung up and gave us the good news. Then Claudia changed the subject. "So Mallory, how's the *Stars of Tomorrow* talent show coming?"

I had been preoccupied with my horse show but I had noticed that the kids seemed pretty organized. "It looks like they're almost ready," I reported. "The triplets helped build a platform in the backyard to use as a stage, and the neighborhood kids have been practicing day and night."

"I bet your mom can hardly wait till the show is over," Mary Anne said with a giggle.

I chuckled. "She's marking the days off on the calendar. Only eight to go."

"So it's really going to happen?" Jessi asked in amazement.

I nodded. "I have to admit that I was skeptical at first, but the kids have organized the show awfully well."

"What about you, Mal?" Stacey asked. "Are you ready for *your* show?"

Her words sent a ripple of fear through me. My shoulders slumped and I stared at the carpet. "I'm as ready as I'll ever be."

Kristy leaned forward in her director's chair and gave me a funny look. "You don't sound very enthusiastic about it."

I hadn't planned to tell my friends just how badly the lessons had been going. I guess I was afraid they would think I was being silly, but suddenly all of these feelings welled up inside me. One second I was looking at the rug on the floor of Claudia's room and the next minute my vision got all blurry. Two tears dropped onto the rug.

Jessi put her hand on my arm. "Mal, what's the matter?"

It was as if a dam had burst inside me and

everything I was worried about came pouring out. I told my friends everything — about my lessons, how much they'd meant to me, and how snobby my classmates had been. Then I told them about the fall.

"Now I'm afraid to get on a horse," I confessed. "Any horse. Even Pax scares me."

"That's all right, Mal," Jessi said softly. "A lot of people are afraid of horses."

"But not me." I bit my lip to stop crying. "I couldn't be. I love them. I mean, it's always been my dream to be a writer and live on a ranch with horses."

"You had a bad fall," Kristy said. "It takes time to get over something like that. Once I was hit in the face by a baseball when I was at bat and it took me nearly a year to stop flinching every time the pitcher threw the ball."

"You think I'll get over it?" I asked, wiping the tears off my cheeks with the back of my hand.

"Of course," Jessi said warmly. "But maybe not right away."

I held my head in my hands. "This is such a mess. I begged my parents to help me pay for lessons. They did, even though I know they really couldn't afford to. And then I had that fall and I spent the next eight lessons clinging to the horse, petrified that I'd fall off again. It was a total waste. I hardly learned anything."

"I'm sure that's not true," Mary Anne said. "I'll bet you've learned a lot and you just don't know it."

Claudia finished the last potato chip and crumpled up the bag. "Frankly, I'm impressed that you're going to be riding a horse with one of those saddles without a handle."

"Handle?" I giggled. "You mean, the saddle horn?"

"That's right." Claudia shook her head. "I don't know how you stay on."

"It's really just a matter of balance and holding on with your knees," I explained with a shrug.

Stacey squeezed my arm. "See? You do know more than you think."

Soon it was six o'clock and time for the meeting to end. Every single member of the BSC wished me luck on Sunday and reminded me that they'd be there to cheer me on. It sure is nice having friends support you.

Jessi suggested we walk our bikes partway home, so we could keep on talking. I was glad she suggested it, because I'd missed her.

"Mal, I had no idea you were so miserable," Jessi said as we neared the corner where we usually split up to go to our own houses.

"I tried to tell you a few times, but you

didn't seem to want to hear about it."

It was Jessi's turn to stare at the ground. "I'm sorry, Mal. I guess I was so jealous of your riding lessons that I could hardly stand to hear about them. Especially when you called and said you'd found your dream horse."

"But he really is a wonderful horse."

"I'm sure he is," Jessi said. "It's just that I thought you were bragging."

I gasped. "I just wanted to share my good news with you."

"You told me you had all these new friends who were rich and owned their own horses," Jessi reminded me. "You told me they invited you to fancy parties with giant video screens and swimming pools."

"Did I really make it sound like that?"

Jessi nodded. "And I felt left out."

"I'm really sorry, Jessi. If you want to know the truth, those new friends barely speak to me. I'm not even sure if they know my name, and we've been together for eight weeks. I don't have the right clothes, I'm the only one who fell off my horse, and I'm the worst rider in the class. The only good thing about the entire two months has been Pax."

Jessi smiled. "He does sound like a wonderful horse."

"Oh, he is!" I cried. "I really want you to meet him."

"I will," Jessi said. "Sunday at the horse show."

"Oh, that." I leaned on my bike's handle-bars. "I really wish I didn't have to go."

"You'll do just fine," Jessi said. "It'll probably only take fifteen minutes, and then all your problems will be solved."

"Not quite," I said. "They're starting another class next week."

Jessi shrugged. "Just don't sign up."

"But how do I explain that to my parents?"

"Tell them the truth. You had a terrible time."

"Oh, Jessi, I could never do that! Mom and Dad couldn't afford to let me take those lessons in the first place, but I begged and pleaded until they gave in. If I tell them I hated the class, they'll feel terrible and I'll look like a jerk."

"Hmmm," Jessi murmured, biting her lip. "That's a tough one. Maybe we should go to my house and talk about it for awhile."

"I can't," I said. "I have to get home for dinner."

"Have dinner with us," Jessi offered.

That was the best thing she could have said. We rode our bikes to her house, and it was just like old times again between us. We had a lot of catching up to do. Eight whole weeks' worth. Jessi and I talked nonstop through dinner. In fact, we had so much to say to each other that I wound up spending the night at her house.

We didn't solve the problem of what to say to my parents about future riding lessons, but right then it didn't matter. Jessi was my best friend again and I felt great.

# CHAPTER 14

The day of the horse show arrived and I was a wreck. From the moment I got out of bed things went wrong. I slept late, I couldn't find my socks, and my hair was out of control. It was humid outside, and my hair looked like a frizzball, even when I tried to smooth it into a ponytail.

The only good thing that happened that morning was that Lauren Kendall stopped by our house. She had borrowed a riding habit from a friend, and she thought it might fit me. The jacket and boots were a little big but I was thrilled anyway.

"There's no sense being the only one in your class riding in jeans," she said. "We're here to put on a show. This will make you look like a real horsewoman."

"Yeah," I thought to myself glumly. "Until I get on the horse."

Actually, I was grateful to Lauren. I had

been so busy worrying about being afraid of horses that I hadn't even thought how I would look in my Western riding clothes.

"Thanks, Lauren," I said as I walked her to the door. "I really appreciate it."

She smiled at me and said, "Be confident today, Mallory. You've got potential."

Her words should have made me feel better, but my nerves had taken over. Mom tried to convince me to eat some breakfast, but my stomach was doing cartwheels and I was afraid I wouldn't be able to keep anything down. All I wanted to do was get out to Kendallwood Farm so I could see Pax and try to relax.

Claire and Margo helped me get dressed — if you could call it help. Claire tried on all the riding gear. She especially liked the boots, which came halfway up her thigh. Margo paraded around in my hunt cap and coat and then tussled with Claire over the riding crop. Finally I managed to wrench the clothing away from my sisters and put it on. I grabbed my mother's hairspray and made a last-ditch effort to de-frizz my hair. It didn't help.

Luckily the phone rang and Adam shouted from the kitchen, "Mal! It's for you!"

"Hi, Mal, it's me," Jessi said when I picked up the phone. "I just wanted to call to wish you luck. In ballet we say break a leg. What do they say in horseback riding?"

"Just the thought of breaking any body parts makes me nervous," I said, laughing. "So 'good luck' would be fine."

"How are you feeling?" Jessi asked.

"Like someone turned on a blender in my stomach."

"That's how I feel before every ballet performance," Jessi said. "But then I make sure I'm very limber and that all my muscles are warmed up. You should do the same."

"You mean, I should do *pliés?*" I asked.

"Yes." Jessi's voice rang with authority. Warming up is one thing she knows everything about. "Do some side stretches," she instructed, "then raise your hands over your head and touch the ground. Then do some slow knee bends."

"I think I can handle that," I said, making a mental list of what she told me to do.

"Then, just before you ride into the ring, take a deep breath and slowly let it out."

"It's funny you should say that," I said. "My teacher, Lauren, is always yelling at us to breathe."

"Well, she's right," Jessi said. "You can't stay loose if you're holding your breath."

Jessi wished me luck a few more times, then Becca had to get on the phone and do the same thing. Finally we hung up, but not before Jessi told me, "Mal, you're my best friend. I'm really proud of you."

Tears stung my eyes (I was turning into a mush, just like Mary Anne) and I mumbled, "Thanks, Jessi. That means a lot to me."

Mom drove me to Kendallwood Farm at eleven o'clock and then went back to the house to get the rest of the family ready. The field in front of the stables was already jammed with cars and horse trailers when my mom dropped me off. I looked at the steady stream of people filing into the bleachers that had been set up around the riding ring and I gulped.

"Now, your dad and I will be back with your brothers and sisters by twelve-thirty," my mother said.

I nodded, barely hearing her. Just the sight of so many cars had started my pulse pounding. I stumbled toward the stable without even waving good-bye.

"Mallory!"

I turned to see what my mother wanted.

"You forgot something." She held up the velvet hunt cap Lauren had brought over that morning.

I shook my head, trying to focus. If I was going to be this ding-y two hours before the show, I could just imagine what I'd be like on horseback in front of a hundred people. A total disaster.

Mom must have noticed the panicked look on my face because she said quietly, "Relax, Mallory. You have plenty of time to get ready. Remember, we're all rooting for you."

I tried to smile confidently but what came out was kind of a sick grimace. After my mom drove away, I hurried as fast as I could through the crowd toward the stable. I heaved a sigh of relief as I slipped inside the dark shadows of Pax's stall and felt his warm, comforting nose nuzzle my neck.

"I am so glad to see you," I whispered, scratching his head behind his ears. "Now it's time to make you pretty."

I tried to braid Pax's mane but he wouldn't hold still to let me work on him. He kept pawing the ground and impatiently nudging the pocket of my jacket. Then I realized what he wanted. His carrot.

"Okay, you win, you big baby," I said, giggling. "Today, because it's an important show, I've brought you a special treat." I pulled two carrots and an apple out of my tote bag. He pressed his muzzle toward them greedily, but I pulled them out of his reach. "Now, don't just inhale them," I said sternly. "I want you to chew."

And he did, dripping apple juice down his

chin. At least it kept him occupied while I braided his mane. Lauren had showed us how to plait the long, thick strands of horsehair, then roll them up and tie them with little satin bows. Soon a neat row of ribbons was lining Pax's neck. Then I curry combed his coat until it glistened.

Pax's tail was harder to untangle than his mane, and also more time consuming, because you aren't supposed to use a comb or brush, just your fingers. I had to separate the strands of hair one by one. But concentrating on the task took my mind off what lay ahead of me — the dreaded horse show.

Finally I saddled and bridled Pax and then stepped back to look at my handiwork. Pax arched his neck and stood proudly, as if he were posing for a picture.

"You already were the most beautiful horse in the stable," I murmured softly. "Now you're the most beautiful in the world."

The blare of a loudspeaker cut through the silence of the stable then, and I heard a voice announce, "Welcome, ladies and gentlemen, to Kendallwood Farm and another splendid afternoon of fine horsemanship from our young riders."

I felt as if someone had thrown a bucket of cold water on me. I left the stall and peeked out the big doors of the barn. The bleachers were full, and I could see my mom and dad in the very last row, with my brothers and sisters lined up in front of them.

Instantly I wanted to run — far, far away, from saddles and bridles and anything having to do with horses or riding.

The speaker crackled again and the announcer said, "Class Number One — that's the pony class — you're on call. Take your mounts to the paddock and warm them up, please. We're now calling the halter class. Will the handlers lead their horses into the ring at once."

Suddenly I couldn't remember when my class — which was Beginning Equitation — was supposed to perform. My throat tightened with panic, and I looked around desperately for someone to ask for help. Behind me Kelsey was leading a chestnut gelding named Brandy out of his stall toward the stable door.

"Kelsey, I don't know when we ride," I gasped. "What am I going to do?"

"Read the schedule, silly," she said, rolling her eyes. "It's tacked to the wall right behind you."

"Oh." I grinned sheepishly. "Thanks."

Kelsey shrugged and left the stable.

I turned and looked at the list of events. So many classes were listed that at first I had trouble finding my own. There were Junior and Senior Jump classes, Hunter Under Saddle (in which the riders showed off their horse's manners), Hunter Over Fences (in which the riders rode their mounts over jumps), and all different levels of Equitation. Finally I saw my own class — Class Three, Beginning Equitation — right after the pony class.

I hurried back to Pax's stall and then led him out of the stable into the bright sunlight. The paddock was full of horses and riders. The halter horses had finished their event and were being led back to the stables.

Now the pony class was entering the ring. The riders, who were about eight years old, were wearing caps, jackets, and high black riding boots like the rest of us. They looked so serious and cute, just like Shirley Temple in the movie *The Little Princess*. That made me think of Jessi, and I scanned the stands for her smiling face. I spotted her at the rail of the show ring. She was surrounded by the entire BSC, and once more my stomach did a flip-flop.

"Beginning Equitation," the loudspeaker blared above my head. "Class Number Three is on call in the paddock."

"That's me," I yelped. I grabbed Pax's reins and led him into the fenced enclosure.

"Mallory," Lauren said as I joined the rest of my class. "You're here. Good."

"I — I'm sorry — " I stammered, but Lauren cut me off.

"Don't worry, you're right on time." Lauren handed each of us a piece of cloth with a number printed on it, and a pair of safety pins. "Attach these to your jackets — top and bottom, please. That's so the judge will be able to tell who's who." Her eyes were bright with excitement. "Now listen, mount your horses and walk them around the paddock. When the announcer calls the class into the ring, enter one at a time and stick to the right. The judge and her assistant — that's the steward — will be standing in the middle of the ring. Once you're all inside, they'll close the gate and put you through your paces. Do *exactly* what the judge says."

Every one of us must have had the same stricken look on our faces because Lauren burst out laughing.

"Don't look so glum! Remember, the judge won't ask you to do anything we haven't done together a hundred times in class. So relax — and *breathe!*"

Twelve nervous riders exhaled at once, and we all started giggling. I walked Pax around the paddock, running over in my mind all the pressure commands for the different gaits. Before I knew it, the loudspeaker was blaring, "We're now calling Class Three, Beginning

Equitation, into the ring. Class Four, Intermediates, are on call."

I followed my class out of the paddock. As we neared the entrance of the show ring, I gave Pax a gentle nudge with my heels. He stepped smartly through the opening, and I found myself staring at a sea of faces.

I heard a wave of applause start at one end of the bleachers and turn into a rushing sound that roared in my ears. Crisp images of the event stick in my mind like little snapshots. My family up in the bleachers, grinning and waving like goons. Jessi and the rest of the BSC on the rail down front, cheering as I passed by. The judge and her assistant standing in the center of the ring, their arms crossed, stern looks on their faces.

After we'd all entered the ring and the gate had been closed behind us, the judge said something to the steward, who gestured toward the announcer's booth.

"Walk your horses, please," the announcer said over the loudspeaker.

We did as we were told. We made a complete circle of the ring and then the steward gestured to the booth again.

"Trot your horses, please."

The judge scribbled furiously on her clipboard while we posted around the ring. I tried my best not to look as clumsy and off balance as I felt. "Heels down, toes up!" I repeated over and over. When we reversed direction, a little voice inside me shouted, "Don't forget your diagonal!"

The announcer then called, "Walk your horses, please."

Pax settled into his comfortable walking pace and I let out a long breath of air. So far, so good.

"Canter your horses, please."

I pressed my knee into Pax's side and he obediently changed gaits. Then the announcer said, "Reverse your horses, please."

Pax turned smartly, but I noticed Kelsey had trouble getting Brandy to take the right lead. I didn't have time to gloat because the announcer was already asking us to come down from the canter to a trot. We returned to a walk and then the announcer told us to line up straight across the arena.

I nudged Pax in beside Allison and prayed that he'd stand still like he was supposed to. Megan was near the front of the line, slumping slightly in her saddle. I noticed the judge make a disapproving face and mark something on her clipboard. I sat up as straight as I could, making sure Pax was square toward the judge, just like Lauren had taught us.

We sat there for what seemed like an eternity. Then the judge handed a note to the steward, who nodded and walked quickly down the line of riders.

"You, you, you, you, you," he said, pointing to Allison and four other riders, including David and Amber. Then he turned to me and added, "And you. Pull out and walk your horses around the ring, please."

I was shocked. Barely thinking, I blindly followed the other horses into the line. The judge made us do everything again, only this time I was the one who goofed up when we reversed directions on the trot. I forgot my diagonal and it took me a second to correct my mistake.

We returned to the lineup and waited anxiously while the judge made a few more notes, then handed her clipboard to the steward, who ran it over to the announcer's booth.

The announcement of the winners came over the loudspeaker: "First place in Beginning Equitation goes to Allison Anders riding Peaches."

The steward pinned a blue ribbon to the bridle of Allison's horse, while the audience applauded. Then the rest of the winners were announced. Amber placed second, a girl named Signe placed third, and David won a pink ribbon for fourth place. Fifth place was announced and then I heard my name blaring out over the speakers: "Sixth place goes to Mallory Pike riding Pax."

The steward pinned a white ribbon on Pax's bridle and then we were done. I couldn't believe it. My butterflies were gone and my worries were over. Pax and I trotted back to the barn like a couple of champions.

"Sixth out of twelve," Jessi said later as she and my brothers and sisters watched me comb down Pax. "That's not bad."

"Not bad?" I groaned. "It's pretty terrible."

"Well, it means half the people in the class were better than you," Vanessa said. "But you were better than the other half."

I laughed. "When you put it that way, it doesn't sound so awful." I spotted my parents making their way toward me from the viewing stands. I whispered to Jessi, "But it's a good excuse for not taking any more riding lessons. Now that they've seen how I ride, they'll know that any more classes would be a waste of money."

Boy, was I wrong about that. My father was beaming when he came into the stable. He scooped me up in his arms and shouted, "Mal, you looked spectacular out there."

"Sixth place." My mother gave me a big hug. "That's pretty darn good for your first show."

"*First* show?" I repeated.

"Of many," my father added.

Mom squeezed my arm. "Your father and I talked it over and we've agreed to cover the full cost of your next eight lessons."

"You'd really do that?" I asked.

"Absolutely." My father draped his arm proudly around my shoulder. "You're a real equestrienne now."

I looked over at Jessi with a sinking feeling. There was no getting around it; I was going to have to tell them the truth. Jessi realized I needed to be alone with my parents, so she bent down and whispered to my brothers and sisters, "How many of you would like to look at the other horses with me?"

Of course they all wanted to. I flashed Jessi a look of thanks and then, taking a deep breath, faced my parents. "Mom. Dad. I have a confession to make."

"What is it, honey?" My mother was still smiling.

I decided to get right to the point. "I really didn't enjoy my lessons very much."

"What?" Dad looked completely surprised.

"After I fell off that horse, I got really scared," I explained. "I had to force myself to go to every lesson. It just wasn't any fun."

"Well, Mal, that's understandable," my mother replied. "But don't you think a few

140

more lessons will help you get over your fear?"

"Maybe later," I said. "But I — I'm just not ready right now."

Mom and Dad exchanged quick glances.

"Mallory, your mother and I don't want to force you to do anything," my father said slowly. "We just thought that since you loved horses so much — "

"Oh, I still do. I'm just not that crazy about *riding* them."

"Are you sure about this?" my mother asked, studying my face.

"I'm positive. The idea of getting on a big horse again really frightens me. Maybe in a couple of years I'll change my mind."

My mother clasped my hand. "I know that must have been difficult to say, Mallory, and we're really pleased you could be so straightforward with us."

"That's right," my father agreed. "And listen, Mallory, if you do change your mind, we'll be ready to help you out. Because frankly, I think you'll make a fine rider someday."

My father spoke so loudly that several of the riders from my class turned to stare and I could feel my cheeks turning bright pink (partly from embarrassment but mostly because I was happy that my parents were so proud of me).

Before I left the farm that afternoon, I asked Jessi to come say good-bye to Pax with me. He was in his stall, happily munching on a bucket of oats. I slipped in beside him and he pressed his muzzle against me. I tried to say good-bye but I couldn't make my mouth form the words. Finally I buried my head in his neck and hugged him for a long time. When I looked up, Jessi was wiping her eyes.

"He really is the most beautiful horse in the world," she said in a soft voice. "You're so lucky to have known him, even if it was for a short time."

"I know," I replied. "I know."

# CHAPTER 15

"It's showtime!" yelled Nicky.

I couldn't help giggling. It was Saturday morning and the *Stars of Tomorrow* talent show was about to begin. Every room in our house was filled with kids putting on makeup or struggling into a costume.

The triplets had volunteered to be the ticket takers in the backyard. Byron kept running through the house making announcements like, "We're really packing 'em in!" or, "I think it's going to be standing room only!"

He was right, too. Our backyard was filled with neighbors, their children, and a couple of dogs and cats. The entire BSC had come to show their support. Several of us were babysitting, so we had brought our charges along. Kristy brought her stepbrother, Andrew, and stepsister, Karen, her brother David Michael, and little Emily Michelle. They took up the entire front row.

Jessi and I sat behind them with Becca and Squirt and Charlotte Johanssen. Dr. Johanssen had called me that morning to see if I would mind watching Charlotte during the talent show. Of course, I said I didn't mind. Charlotte and Becca were just about the only kids in our neighborhood who weren't going to be in the *Stars of Tomorrow* talent show. But they had been adamant about not doing it. After their miserable experiences in the Little Miss Stoneybrook contest, both of them had sworn they would never appear on the stage again. But they made very enthusiastic audience members.

"Bring on the stars!" Becca shouted, clapping her hands.

Several older kids in the audience heard her cry and started clapping and chanting, "We want a show! We want a show!"

A dismayed look crossed Nicky's face, and he ducked behind the curtains to confer with Vanessa. The curtains were still just blankets, only now big silver stars made of aluminum foil were pinned to them.

The triplets decided to do some crowd control. They ran to the front of the stage and yelled, "Quiet! *Quiet! SHUT UP!"*

"I knew their loud mouths were good for something," I said, giggling, to Jessi.

Vanessa stepped through the curtains,

dressed in white tights and my dad's tuxedo jacket and bow tie. "Welcome to the first annual *Stars of Tomorrow* talent show," she declared, "brought to you by the one and only Pike family."

A cheer sounded from the triplets, who had taken up positions around the audience to make sure there were no hecklers. Then Vanessa gestured grandly to her right.

Nothing happened.

Finally she cupped her hands around her mouth and hissed, "Margo. You're on."

Margo stuck her head around the side of the curtains and blinked. "Now?"

Vanessa rolled her eyes and put her hands on her hips. "Yes. Now."

This sent a wave of laughter through the audience. At first Margo looked shocked and then she started giggling, too. In fact, she was laughing so hard she couldn't read the piece of paper she held in her hand.

Finally Vanessa marched over to her side and said, "Give me that." Vanessa studied the paper and announced, "Our first act will be Sean Addison on the tuba."

Nicky stuck his head through the curtains and called, "Sean can't find his tuba. He's back here crying."

"Well, help him find it," Vanessa shot back, "and tell Buddy's he's on."

"I think I saw Sean's tuba in the kitchen," I whispered to Jessi. "I'll go get it."

Jessi nodded. "Okay. And I'll go help Sean."

We left Becca, Squirt, and Charlotte seated on the grass. They were applauding wildly as a gray cat bolted across the stage, pursued by Pow the basset hound. Buddy and Suzi Barrett were both gripping his leash but weren't having any luck getting him to stop.

"Hey!" Nicky shouted to them. "You're not supposed to come on till after you're introduced."

Buddy ignored Nicky and just kept tugging on the leash. "Stop it, Pow," he bellowed. "I mean it."

Luckily the cat made a quick exit through a hedge and Pow's leash caught on a tree by the stage.

Buddy didn't seemed to be flustered at all. With a big grin on his face he turned to the crowd and announced, "I'm Buddy Barrett and this is my dog Pow, the fastest dog in the West. He also talks. Want to hear him?"

"Yes!" the audience shouted.

I made my way through the costumed kids who were clustered on our back porch and stepped inside the empty house. Sean's tuba was just where he'd left it that morning — on the kitchen table. I picked it up and, after a quick look around to make sure no other instruments or costumes had been left behind, hurried back outside.

Buddy and Pow were just completing their jump-through-the-hula-hoop trick. To make sure Pow would make his leap through the hoop, Buddy had brought a large T-bone steak with him. I secretly wondered if Buddy's mother knew what her son was using as bait.

Pow bounded through the hoop without any urging and promptly settled down to devour his steak. No amount of urging could get him to budge from his spot. Finally the triplets rushed to Buddy's aid and the three of them dragged Pow, his steak clasped firmly between his teeth, off the stage.

The audience cheered and, while Vanessa waited for them to quiet down so she could announce the next act, I scanned the crowd. I was truly amazed at the turnout. People were still entering the yard. I spotted Dawn as she paid her admittance. She was carrying Eleanor Marshall on her hip and holding Nina's hand. Dawn waved to me and I grinned back. After passing the tuba to Claire, who quickly took it backstage, I hurried over to say hello.

"Mow-ree!" Eleanor squealed.

"How's the show going?" Dawn asked, flipping her sunglasses to the top of her head.

"It got off to kind of a rocky start," I said

with a grin. "But now it looks like it's going to be a success."

I felt a tug on my sleeve and saw Nina grinning up at me. "Mallory," she said. "Guess what."

I knelt down beside her. "I give up. What?"

"I brought Blankie to the show today."

"Blankie?" I looked up at Dawn, who nodded.

"He's in the front pocket of her shirt," Dawn whispered.

Nina beamed proudly and patted the pocket. "But nobody knows except you and Dawn and Eleanor. It's our secret."

I pretended to pull a zipper across my mouth. "Don't worry," I promised. "I won't tell a soul."

"*Ooooh!*" the crowd suddenly murmured. I turned to see what the commotion was about and was startled to see Nicky's head towering four feet above the clothesline.

"He's on stilts," Dawn cried. "I didn't know he could do that."

"Neither did I," I said in amazement. My brother, sporting a red, white, and blue top hat and a white goatee beard, grinned at the audience as my sister announced, "And now, let's hear it for Nicholas Pike as Uncle Sam."

"Yankee Doodle Dandy" blasted out of the tape recorder as Nicky strutted back and forth in front of the curtains on his stilts. He was wearing a long pair of pants that completely covered the wooden stilts, so he truly seemed to be an eight-foot-tall person.

"Hasn't Nicky been practicing at home?" Dawn asked me.

I shrugged. "He might have been, but I was kind of preoccupied with my riding lessons and the horse show and everything."

My lessons really had taken up a big chunk of my time. I'd neglected my friendship with the members of the Baby-sitters Club, especially Jessi, and with my own brothers and sisters. But that was over now and I was relieved. Jessi was my best friend again and horses were just a small part of my life again. Kind of like Nina and her Blankie. She no longer needed to carry the big cumbersome blanket around with her. A small piece of it was just fine. And loving horses from a distance was fine enough for me.

Finally all of the *Stars of Tomorrow* performers took their curtain calls. As Vanessa, Margo, Claire, and Nicky stepped forward to take their bows, everyone cheered.

But nobody cheered louder than me.

## About the Author

ANN M. MARTIN did *a lot* of baby-sitting when she was growing up in Princeton, New Jersey. She is a former editor of books for children, and was graduated from Smith College.

Ms. Martin lives in New York City with her cats, Mouse and Rosie. She likes ice cream and *I Love Lucy;* and she hates to cook.

Ann Martin's Apple Paperbacks include *Yours Turly, Shirley; Ten Kids, No Pets; With You and Without You; Bummer Summer;* and all the other books in the Baby-sitters Club series.

Look for #55

## JESSI'S GOLD MEDAL

On Thursday I felt more excited than nervous. But still, when I showed up at the pool complex during fourth period, my stomach was rumbling.

It was a little embarrassing, I have to admit — and I couldn't figure out why it was happening. After all, I'm used to performing in front of crowds.

Then I realized my poor little stomach was being faked out. Usually fourth period meant lunch — no wonder it was complaining.

I saw Ms. Cox running toward me (maybe she heard the rumbling). "Jessi, hi!" she called out.

"Hi," I said.

Ms. Cox turned around and said in a loud voice, "Girls! We have someone new in the class — Jessica Ramsey. Jessi, this is Abby, Monica, Hannah . . ."

She mentioned fifteen names altogether,

151

and after she was done I didn't remember one name. I guess I *was* nervous.

"Hi," I said again and again. I was really showing off my vocabulary, huh?

"Oh, this is wonderful," Ms. Cox went on. "We finally have an even number in the class. You see, Jessi, we do a lot of work in pairs. With only fifteen girls, that means someone is always switching around. Right, Elise?"

A pretty, raven-haired girl smiled and said, "Yep."

"Elise Coates has been partners with just about everyone in the class," Ms. Cox went on. "But not any more. I'm going to assign you two to be a permanent pair, okay? I think you guys'll do great together. Take a few minutes, get to know each other, and then Elise can catch you up on some basics." She turned to Elise and said, "Go over the sidestroke and the crawl, and show her the standard scull, the tub position, and maybe the tub turn and the back tuck somersault if you have time. I'll be around to help you out."

Huh?

Tub turn? Back tuck somersault? What had I gotten myself into?

**Don't miss any of the latest books
in the Baby-sitters Club series
by Ann M. Martin**

#51 *Stacey's Ex-Best Friend*
Is Stacey's old friend Laine super mature or just a
super snob?

#52 *Mary Anne + 2 Many Babies*
Who ever thought taking care of a bunch of babies
could be so much trouble?

#53 *Kristy for President*
Can Kristy run the BSC and the whole eighth
grade?

Super Specials:
# 6 *New York, New York!*
Bloomingdales, the Hard Rock Cafe — the BSC is
going to see it all!

# 7 *Snowbound*
Stoneybrook gets hit by a major blizzard. Will the
baby-sitters be o.k.?

Mysteries:
# 3 *Mallory and the Ghost Cat*
Mallory finds a spooky white cat. Could it be a
ghost?

# 4 *Kristy and the Missing Child*
Kristy organizes a search party to help the police
find a missing child.

# 5 *Mary Anne and the Secret in the Attic*
Mary Anne uncovers a secret from her past and
now she's afraid of her future!

## by Ann M. Martin

| | | | |
|---|---|---|---|
| ☐ MG43388-1 | #1 | Kristy's Great Idea | $3.25 |
| ☐ MG43513-2 | #2 | Claudia and the Phantom Phone Calls | $3.25 |
| ☐ MG43511-6 | #3 | The Truth About Stacey | $3.25 |
| ☐ MG43512-4 | #4 | Mary Anne Saves the Day | $3.25 |
| ☐ MG43720-8 | #5 | Dawn and the Impossible Three | $3.25 |
| ☐ MG43899-9 | #6 | Kristy's Big Day | $3.25 |
| ☐ MG43719-4 | #7 | Claudia and Mean Janine | $3.25 |
| ☐ MG43509-4 | #8 | Boy-Crazy Stacey | $3.25 |
| ☐ MG43508-6 | #9 | The Ghost at Dawn's House | $3.25 |
| ☐ MG43387-3 | #10 | Logan Likes Mary Anne! | $3.25 |
| ☐ MG43660-0 | #11 | Kristy and the Snobs | $3.25 |
| ☐ MG43721-6 | #12 | Claudia and the New Girl | $3.25 |
| ☐ MG43386-5 | #13 | Good-bye Stacey, Good-bye | $3.25 |
| ☐ MG43385-7 | #14 | Hello, Mallory | $3.25 |
| ☐ MG43717-8 | #15 | Little Miss Stoneybrook...and Dawn | $3.25 |
| ☐ MG44234-1 | #16 | Jessi's Secret Language | $3.25 |
| ☐ MG43659-7 | #17 | Mary Anne's Bad-Luck Mystery | $2.95 |
| ☐ MG43718-6 | #18 | Stacey's Mistake | $3.25 |
| ☐ MG43510-8 | #19 | Claudia and the Bad Joke | $3.25 |
| ☐ MG43722-4 | #20 | Kristy and the Walking Disaster | $3.25 |
| ☐ MG43507-8 | #21 | Mallory and the Trouble with Twins | $2.95 |
| ☐ MG43658-9 | #22 | Jessi Ramsey, Pet-sitter | $3.25 |
| ☐ MG43900-6 | #23 | Dawn on the Coast | $3.25 |
| ☐ MG43506-X | #24 | Kristy and the Mother's Day Surprise | $3.25 |
| ☐ MG43347-4 | #25 | Mary Anne and the Search for Tigger | $3.25 |
| ☐ MG42503-X | #26 | Claudia and the Sad Good-bye | $3.25 |
| ☐ MG42502-1 | #27 | Jessi and the Superbrat | $2.95 |
| ☐ MG42501-3 | #28 | Welcome Back, Stacey! | $2.95 |
| ☐ MG42500-5 | #29 | Mallory and the Mystery Diary | $3.25 |
| ☐ MG42498-X | #30 | Mary Anne and the Great Romance | $3.25 |
| ☐ MG42497-1 | #31 | Dawn's Wicked Stepsister | $3.25 |
| ☐ MG42496-3 | #32 | Kristy and the Secret of Susan | $2.95 |
| ☐ MG42495-5 | #33 | Claudia and the Great Search | $2.95 |
| ☐ MG42494-7 | #34 | Mary Anne and Too Many Boys | $2.95 |

*More titles...* ▶

*The Baby-sitters Club titles continued...*

| | | |
|---|---|---|
| ❑ MG42508-0 | #35 Stacey and the Mystery of Stoneybrook | $2.95 |
| ❑ MG43565-5 | #36 Jessi's Baby-sitter | $2.95 |
| ❑ MG43566-3 | #37 Dawn and the Older Boy | $3.25 |
| ❑ MG43567-1 | #38 Kristy's Mystery Admirer | $3.25 |
| ❑ MG43568-X | #39 Poor Mallory! | $3.25 |
| ❑ MG44082-9 | #40 Claudia and the Middle School Mystery | $3.25 |
| ❑ MG43570-1 | #41 Mary Anne Versus Logan | $2.95 |
| ❑ MG44083-7 | #42 Jessi and the Dance School Phantom | $3.25 |
| ❑ MG43572-8 | #43 Stacey's Emergency | $3.25 |
| ❑ MG43573-6 | #44 Dawn and the Big Sleepover | $2.95 |
| ❑ MG43574-4 | #45 Kristy and the Baby Parade | $3.25 |
| ❑ MG43569-8 | #46 Mary Anne Misses Logan | $3.25 |
| ❑ MG44971-0 | #47 Mallory on Strike | $3.25 |
| ❑ MG43571-X | #48 Jessi's Wish | $3.25 |
| ❑ MG44970-2 | #49 Claudia and the Genius of Elm Street | $3.25 |
| ❑ MG44969-9 | #50 Dawn's Big Date | $3.25 |
| ❑ MG44968-0 | #51 Stacey's Ex-Best Friend | $3.25 |
| ❑ MG44966-4 | #52 Mary Anne + 2 Many Babies | $3.25 |
| ❑ MG44967-2 | #53 Kristy for President | $3.25 |
| ❑ MG44965-6 | #54 Mallory and the Dream Horse | $3.25 |
| ❑ MG44964-8 | #55 Jessi's Gold Medal | $3.25 |
| ❑ MG45575-3 | Logan's Story  Special Edition Readers' Request | $3.25 |
| ❑ MG44240-6 | Baby-sitters on Board!  Super Special #1 | $3.50 |
| ❑ MG44239-2 | Baby-sitters' Summer Vacation  Super Special #2 | $3.50 |
| ❑ MG43973-1 | Baby-sitters' Winter Vacation  Super Special #3 | $3.50 |
| ❑ MG42493-9 | Baby-sitters' Island Adventure  Super Special #4 | $3.50 |
| ❑ MG43575-2 | California Girls!  Super Special #5 | $3.50 |
| ❑ MG43576-0 | New York, New York!  Super Special #6 | $3.50 |
| ❑ MG44963-X | Snowbound  Super Special #7 | $3.50 |

Available wherever you buy books...or use this order form.

Scholastic Inc., P.O. Box 7502, 2931 E. McCarty Street, Jefferson City, MO 65102

Please send me the books I have checked above. I am enclosing $_____ (please add $2.00 to cover shipping and handling). Send check or money order - no cash or C.O.D.s please.

Name _____

Address _____

City_____ State/Zip _____

Please allow four to six weeks for delivery. Offer good in the U.S. only. Sorry, mail orders are not available to residents of Canada. Prices subject to change.